The Haunting of Hacket House

By

Astrid Addams

From the same author

The Man

The Haunting of Hope House

Clive was certain. Well as certain as he ever was about anything. He'd seen the evil with his own eyes after all, but could he really trust them? Here in the darkness as he peered by the light of the torch shaking in his hand, he couldn't be sure, or so he told himself as he crept down yet another corridor in his childhood home. Even as a small boy he had hated it. He'd never been a man who believed in Gods, never felt the presence of the big G at his side, but now, in the hungry darkness, he simultaneously cursed whatever other forces may be out there for bringing him back here, for wedging Hacket House into his family history like a splinter into flesh. Simultaneously still he prayed to the same Gods to get him and Clarissa away, anywhere would do as long as it was away from this hellish place. 'When the shit hits the fan, that's when having a God to pray to or curse is really satisfying,' his mother used to tell him between drags of her cigarette.

Clive stood still and strained his ears, listening for the sounds of creaking floorboards. His legacy! Eaten alive by woodworm and haunted by the never-ending ticking of clocks which served to mask the sound of whatever evil might be coming. As satisfied as he thought he'd ever be, Clive began his slow creeping once again. He had to find his and Clarissa's room, tell her what he'd seen, do whatever it took to convince her that they had to leave this house to the worms and the rot and get out, go home and forget this place even existed. The old man was dead and he could rot in his grand bedroom surrounded by his precious clocks, the clocks that used to give Clive nightmares well after his mother had left his father and taken him with her. Far away, to a house with only digital silent clocks. She'd died a few months back, her death had hit him hard, and it had been Clarissa's idea to come here, to patch things up with his old man. To see if he'd lend them the money needed to save them from bankruptcy. What they'd found once they'd arrived was a decrepit house and an even more decrepit man who was completely mad. At least that is what Clive and Clarissa had thought at the time. He suspected differently now, even if he dare not believe what he suspected yet.

He'd found the library and its secrets last night on his way to the bathroom. He hadn't believed them, not really, who the hell would? He'd paced the floor, running his hands through his too long hair, wondering what the hell to do to quiet his mind and reassure himself that it really was just suppositious ramblings. The stories people made up when scientific discovery was just too boring an explanation for earthquakes and a God with a giant hammer or a piece of pissed off real estate with a score to settle was far more interesting. Some were probably just malicious pieces of tat used to justify human suffering and frighten people into following some religious cult, pouring money into the pockets of their fat, syphilitic holy men and women. Though that didn't quite feel right either. Nothing rational felt right at Hacket House and what he'd found tonight was no exception. What was documented in the somehow still brilliant scarlet ink on the ancient pages, part organza, part parchment, did not fit with any religion he'd ever heard of. Not just ancient pages either, some of the paper and writings were unnervingly recent. There had to have been a number of people developing serious mental health problems in the house or the community, only they didn't know what mental illness was back then so they blamed evil spirits or witches or black goats. This Nark was probably just some creepy old dude no one liked who scared the children, so when grandma got dementia who was blamed? This Nark of course.

The community had seemed backwards to Clive even as a kid; they had probably believed in witches and boogie men well after the rest of the country had moved on. Clive shuddered at the thought of boogie men. He had a feeling that out of all the crazy thoughts flying round his skull, that Nark's continuing influence was the only correct one. Even having covered the watching grandfather clock and paced the room for so long that he feared ruining the carpet, the discomfort he couldn't explain remained. Eventually he knew what he must do, he'd peek in on his father, just quickly so as not to wake him, and then he'd know both it and Nark was just a load of nonsense. If only the house wasn't such a maze and he could find it.

As his thoughts rambled on, Clive reached the end of the corridor and peered around the corner. In the shaking torch light, a tall figure loomed against the wall, and Clive's scream caught in his throat. He felt his windpipe constrict, the dead fish that had once been his tongue flopped around uselessly. For a few seconds all he could think was that he was going to be joining his father, then the big clock chimed and Clive almost chocked on his own tongue. This was their corridor, it had to be, please God it had to be. The warped floor creaked under him and Clive's short-lived relief evaporated. His and Clarissa's corridor was not warped and did not creak when you stepped onto it. Clive cursed under his breath and he felt as if he would cry. He needed Clarissa beside him, she'd been beside him ever since his first day at university almost ten years ago. Eighteen and nervous, he'd run into her at the freshers fair and she had talked him into joining the atheists society. She was the fresh air in his life and now the backbone, the wall that propped him up, padded and kind, supporting him to make most of the decisions he made every day from the smallest to the largest. She knew he'd be lost without her and he knew it too. And now he was lost and alone, feeling sorry for himself in his father's house. His father had paid for him to go to university and Clive had never had the chance to thank him. Now he never would because the old man was lying dead in his four-poster bed, surrounded by his precious clocks and long velvet drapery.

The light in Clive's hand shook violently, threatening to fall from his limp wrist and crash to the floor. His father had not been alone when he called in on him. Clive swallowed hard and tried to fight away the image of the gnarled twisted thing, crawling on the rug beside the bed. Like the largest and ugliest dog in existence. But it hadn't been a dog, it was transparent, with a yellow tinge, and Clive was certain that it had come from his father's gaping black hole of a mouth. He tried to fight off the image of the cruel, twisted human face that snapped around to face him and let out a low growl. Something changed, a small movement, an almost inaudible sound, a small breeze maybe, Clive wasn't sure. Gooseflesh erupted, a whimper escaped Clive's dry lips, and he was off, running down the corridor, too terrified to move quietly. Hell, if he made enough noise, Clarissa, the sullen handy man, or that lazy bitch of a carer might come and find him! He only hoped that they'd find him before the other did.

Suddenly Clive was flat against a wall, the wall humming against his flesh. God, what kind of parasites lived in this hell hole? Winded by the impact, he fell back gasping as the wall slid to the side and a low growl sounded from the other end of the corridor. Clive didn't look around to see as he dove into the unexpected safe haven and, as he clicked his flashlight off, he heard the wall slide shut behind him. The total darkness was far worse than the semi darkness his little light cast and Clive stood holding his breath, not moving. Every nerve felt alive, ready to run at the slightest touch or sound. Clive listened and remained as still as he could, hoping his eyes would adjust to the dark, but they didn't. All he could hear was the usual steady ticking of a nearby clock. Did the clock mask its growls? Was that why his father and grandfather had wasted their lives building them? It was a crazy thought, but one Clive could easily buy.

Clive remained how he was, debating what to do and wondering if it was safe enough to turn the little light on. Under normal circumstances he would have asked Clarissa, but this was anything but normal. Eventually, when he could stand the dark no longer, his trembling thumb flicked the switch. Clive let out a strangled cry, finding himself back in his father's room, looking at the man, who sat up in bed, milky eyes and toothless mouth wide open and staring at him. Clive stepped backwards away from the corpse and that's when he heard the low growl coming from the darkness.

Three Years Later

Chapter 1

It was another grey and dreary day. The perfect day for a long train journey, Jane thought as she stared at the rich green hills and fields flying past her. She liked to watch the world fly by like this, as if she was detached from it in the cocoon of the second-class carriage. If only she was on her way to a new life, somewhere hot and exotic and alien. Jane sighed against the glass, it was mid-morning and Jane wanted a coffee but not enough to put her hand in her pocket and buy one. She had been up half the night in anxiety of the journey and, most of all, the dead-end village where she was heading. The music from the phone that never rang, tiredness, and the greenery mixed together to create a rather pleasant psychedelic stupor as Jefferson Airplane sang her favourite song and Jane followed the call of the 'hookah-smoking caterpillar, remembering her mum's own voice singing along. White Rabbit was her mum's favourite song too; Jane remembered her singing it continuously as she washed up or cooked, swinging her hips to the imaginary rhythm as the smells of whatever she was doing wafted through the air. She'd passed it on to her daughter and Jane still felt that jobs were only done well, and food was only ever really good, if cooked to the tune of White Rabbit by Jefferson Airplane.

When the train hit a tunnel the spell was broken, and Jane dragged herself from the window and retrieved her documents from her bag. For the hundredth time she removed the now dog-eared letter from its envelope and unfolded the creases. The letter was written on thick, rich-textured paper which gave the impression of stuffy wealth and she read the address again - Hacket House. An unpleasant, unforgiving sort of name that brought forth thoughts of illness and disgusting colds, but what was in a name? She'd looked it up online, or tried to, but according to the usually infallible internet, neither Hacket House, nor the nearest village Bramley, existed. A major anxiety for Jane, even when she'd been offered the role and assured that there had been no mistake. It really was Hacket House, one and a half miles outside the village of Bramley, they just kept a low profile, that's all.

"It's lovely country here, we don't want it crawling with tourists you know," the cheery woman had explained over the phone when Jane had called the number given. Nevertheless, a significantly large check, now cashed and sat in her bank account, had been required before she had handed her notice in with her company just over a week ago.

She was going to Hacket House to be a live-in carer for a gentleman called Tobias Smithson, according to the documents she had been sent by the housekeeper, which she had read almost compulsively. It sounded like caring for Mr Smithson would be an easy job. Whilst he did have dementia, it was the end stages and the old man was apparently bed bound, unable to talk, unable to feed himself or do anything except stare into space and cry out. A phenomenon Jane secretly thought of as the dementia rattle. What was important to Jane was that it meant no endless wandering, attempts to get into bed with her, or impossible to answer questions and mind games. More importantly still, the old man was apparently relatively docile. No lashing out, spitting or attempting to claw the flesh from her arms when she worked to prevent pressure sores or the skin deterioration known in children as nappy rash. Compared to some of the people with dementia she had known he sounded positively angelic.

For the last three years, Jane had been a livein carer for a never-ending series of wealthy elderly people. The kind of old people who'd inherited wealth or enjoyed really good jobs with healthy pensions, the type of which Jane knew she'd never get to enjoy. Some of them she still missed and thought about, one of whom she would have stayed with forever if he hadn't passed away one night. Others haunted her, in the night as she laid in the dark in yet another unfamiliar room, she'd think she heard Millie's sticks taping down the corridor, or the shouting of Edward. Sometimes she'd wake with a start, certain the mattress beside her had moved and that Ronald was once again getting into bed beside her. More disturbingly than a strange old man climbing into bed with her was the knowledge he was doing it thinking that she was his wife.

Walking through unfamiliar houses she'd see a shadow or sense a presence and spin around, expecting to see Edgar creeping about behind her in his bare feet. Instead she'd find nothing but shadows and over the top furniture. It had never been Edgar, not in the eleven months since she'd left his house in the middle of one pouring night after waking to find Edgar's hands around her throat. She'd heard from his daughter when she'd called her in a panic that he'd attempted to do the same thing to his wife before she'd moved into residential care. Apparently, her company was meant to have warned her, but when she challenged them about it, they denied any knowledge of Edgar's history.

She had been living with a sweet lady called May, whose son had followed his father into investment banking and who had herself been a teacher, but who now spent most of the day roaming her house or sat staring into space with a vacant smile. She rarely spoke unless spoken to, but she was always in a good mood. Jane had done everything, all care and housework and washing. She was doing the washing one day when she found out about the job at Hacket House. Whilst she was hanging out the washing, May's neighbour, a Mrs Jonas, came out with a newspaper. They had got talking when Jane moved in and had become friendly acquaintances. Mrs Jonas had seen something in one of the papers sent to her by her son that she thought Jane might be interested in. Jane quickly saw it was a job advert for a live-in carer offering over double the pay she was currently getting. May's sons were in the process of securing a nursing home placement for May, Jane suspected that they were hoping to get the house, so Jane applied. She couldn't believe it when she found out that her application had been successful and that the service user would be so easy to look after. Best of all she wouldn't be living alone with them so she'd have some normal company. Sometimes the loneliness would get too much, and Jane would wonder if she was losing her mind or if she had really fallen down some rabbit hole or other.

It was a long train journey with few stops, a direct train because Jane didn't like changing trains and the ticket had been paid for without hesitation or question by her new employer. Most of the journey was through rolling green fields and steeply sloping green hills with nothing but ancient stone farmhouses. The odd sheep or cows completely ignored the train shooting past. A couple of times she'd seen vast and deep reservoirs of grey. Jane found the monotony and the rhythmic clacking of the train soothing and she started to drift in and out of a pleasant, dreamlike state. Around her the number of passengers started to dwindle with every infrequent stop until at last Jane was alone.

In five short hours Jane found herself rolling the small battered suitcase she'd found in a skip towards the doors of the slowing train. What sun there had been was getting ready to retire into what promised to become a deep blue evening as Jane stepped onto the pretty, but dead end, platform with only an ancient, boarded up building and green trees. From her letter she knew that Bramley village was nearby, but she couldn't see it as she walked along the deserted platform, the suitcase snapping at her heels as she headed through the exit to the country lane beside the platform. Something tightened in her throat as she looked from side to side and found that the promised car that would take her to her new job was not there waiting for her. In fact, she was completely alone as the light began to change and the shadows seemed to grow around her.

Chapter 2

With nothing else to do but inwardly curse that her phone had no signal, Jane stood at the edge of the green lane and waited. Nerves crept around her in the air and skulked in trees that hung over both sides of the pathless road. Jane really didn't want to be there by the time darkness started to creep over the world. She wished she had not worn her best peach coloured dress and long cream coat. She had wanted to make a good impression when she arrived, but at half five in the middle of nowhere all she felt was self-conscious. Her foot, in its sensible flat but glossy shoe, tapped the uneven concrete as she fought the urge to start pacing, even though there was no one around to see her. The minutes dragged by as Jane became more and more convinced that something was very wrong, that she had been tricked into a trap of some sort. Her throat grew tighter and tighter and she wrapped her arms around herself, scanning one side of the road and then the other. Then she scanned the trees more closely, searching for him. Visions of him, action man like, dressed in black with binoculars and perched in a tree, played through her mind as they tended to at moments like this. She wondered how the hell he'd managed to find her despite everything she'd done. Maybe he wasn't alone. He was good at getting people on his side, twisting their spines around his little finger, making people believe his version of events. It was his greatest strength, that easy going charm that sucked you in and made you believe that no, he couldn't possibly do something so despicable. No matter what anybody else or other evidence said. Jane, however, had learnt the hard way, that unspeakable evil lived behind that pretty face and mask of charm. Why did people have to be so gullible when faced with a pretty face and a charming smile?

Just as the familiar monster of fear was about to rear its ugly head, a pair of headlights turned onto the little road, casting two dim orange arcs of colour over her and the concrete. Jane smoothed her coat and strained her eyes, praying silently that it was the promised car. The car crept nearer, and she saw it was large and vintage, a posh one with plenty of room in the back and probably leather seats. The kind of car that might be used for weddings except that its shape was ugly and its shiny paintwork was black. Relief and suspicion fought for prominence as the car pulled up before her and a tall, stern-looking man in a black suit stepped out.

'Miss Jane Elliot?' the man asked in a curt, clear voice, his worn face and greying dark hair putting him at between forty and fifty. He reminded Jane of Liam Neeson, especially when he did not smile.

'Yes,' Jane heard herself squeak.

'I'm Atticus Whiteley, I'm the maintenance man at Hacket House,' Mr Whiteley informed her as he moved around the car, advancing on Jane. When he was at her side, he bent forwards, a movement that did not suit him, and held open the passenger door.

'I'll put your luggage in the boot. Where is the rest of it?'

Jane swallowed 'This is it, I.... like to travel light.'

Embarrassed, Jane hopped into the car, noting that the seats were leather after all, and fastened her seatbelt. In a moment Mr Whiteley was beside her in the driver's seat and the engine roared to life. Her brief meeting with Mr Whiteley had convinced Jane that the journey would be long and silent in the changing light. However as soon as they pulled away, Mr Whiteley addressed her.

'So, you're going to be Mr Smithson's new live-in nurse?'

'Live-in carer. I do the dirty work without the degree.' Jane didn't turn to face Mr Whiteley as she stared out of the window at the trees and the winding country lanes.

'You done this before? You know what to expect?'

'I've cared for people with dementia before and been a live-in a carer for over two years now. The housekeeper wrote to me about all his care needs.'

'What do you know about Mr Smithson and the house?'

'Not much, I couldn't find the house on Google Maps and I don't see how knowing what Mr Smithson did will help me look after him now. I'm sure your housekeeper can tell me more about anything he likes or doesn't like.'

'Didn't she tell you that the house is meant to be haunted?'

Jane felt herself shiver and the black shadows of the trees seemed to close in tighter around the car.

'Most nursing homes are meant to be haunted, I used to work nights and not once did I see a ghost or anything supernatural.'

Mr Whiteley's laugh was harsh, brittle and forced.

'Yeah, well, Hacket House is no ordinary haunted house. The stories go back hundreds of years, to well before that fool Arthur Hacket built a house on the land. When you get there you'll see it's wood. Have you ever seen a wooden house? Rumour has it that nothing else would stay upright long enough to be christened a house. The local villagers believe the land it is built on is the devil's own. Mr Smithson believed it too, before the confusion set in. The old timers at the pub say Smithson doesn't really have dementia, that it's a sort of madness.'

'What do you believe?' Jane said to the undergrowth before turning to face the driver.

Mr Whiteley threw back his head and laughed. A deep, natural chuckle that seemed to last for far too long. Mr Whiteley's face was not a face naturally suited for laughter and the effect was distinctly unsettling.

'About ten years ago my wife passed away.'

'Oh, I'm so sorry I-' Mr Whiteley held up a hand and continued.

'I wasn't, it wasn't a happy marriage, but we lived on the grounds together all our married life and I still live in our little cottage. It's different from the normal type, the kind our ancestors froze in and rich people buy up for long weekends so that the next generation can't live in the village they grew up in. Like the house, it's made of wood from the land. But it's a pretty cottage, the wife was dead proud of it, definitely preferred it to me. It's a perk of the job, has its own generator and water supply, everything the house has really. She died there, found her dead one day face down on the hard floor. Looked like she'd been mopping, then slipped on the wet floor and cracked her skull on the edge of the mantelpiece. At least that's what the coroner said. You know how many times she's been back to see me and bollock me for wearing my boots indoors and getting mud on her clean floors?'

'Well no.'

'Never, she has never been back to visit me or the house she loved more than she ever loved me. Believe me, if she'd been able to come back and carry on making my life a misery, she would have.'

Jane shivered, not just at the edge in the man's voice, but at the unpleasant memories his words stirred up. Memories that threatened to join them in the now silent car. Mr Whiteley rounded a bend Jane didn't see coming and she found herself facing a large iron gate at least seven feet tall, comprising of intricate iron swirls and coils. It was a deliberately grand and spectacular sight, only marred by the rust creeping over the once black paintwork.

Suddenly the car stopped and Mr Whiteley turned to face her. His face was creased in a deep frown.

'Well, how're you feeling?' he asked.

'Nervous I suppose. It's always weird going somewhere new.' Jane turned back to the gate.

'You don't feel… ill or anything? No pains?'

'No, I'm fine really. Do I look ill?' Jane suddenly wished she had her mirror as a wave of self-consciousness hit her.

'No you don't. It's just, well, some people get car sick on these winding roads and the bumpy suspension in this thing doesn't help.

'No really, I'm fine thank you.'

Chapter 3

Atticus Whiteley got out of the car and unlocked the large chain and padlock holding the gate shut. Jane looked out of her window at a large wooden sign with golden letters. Despite the shadows from the overhanging undergrowth and the fading light, Jane was able to read the lettering.

'Warning! Private Property! Trespassers and poachers will be prosecuted.'

'Friendly welcome isn't it?' Jane said as Mr Whiteley climbed back into the driver's seat.

Mr Whiteley shook his head.

'Anyone who is thick enough to trespass here never stays long.'

Jane wasn't sure how best to respond, so said nothing as Mr Whiteley drove through the gates.

They started the long, curved drive up through woods, then past wild hedgerows and bushes twisted into unnatural spikes and dislocated so that their limbs bent in odd directions as if they had been tortured by some unknown force. What was stranger still was the colour of the wood and the leaves. No matter what specie of tree or bush Jane looked at, they all had the same deep red bark, the colour of dried clotted blood just before a thick scab is formed. The leaves were lighter reds, like fresh blood or scarlet, sometimes even burgundy. It seemed to Jane that the bushes and trees were somehow living creatures. That when she looked away, they would move, and when she looked back they would be watching her. She felt sure that if she got out of the car and placed her hand on the rough bark of one of the trees that she would feel the plants' pulse pumping away. She was equally sure that someone else was watching them, the hairs on the back of her neck, erect like tiny antennas, told her so. She dared not look away during what seemed to be an excessively long drive, and Jane wondered if they'd ever make it to the house. Suddenly it was in front of them and Jane gasped.

It was like no other house she had ever seen. For starters it appeared to be made out of wood, but a lighter red than the trees it came from where the bark had been stripped away. The structure comprised of a number of towers and intricately carved pillars. In the centre of the house, above the front door, was the face of a large clock. As they drove forwards Jane was able to see that the house appeared to be crawling with black vines that seemed to hold it in place like a straitjacket, forcing the clock to remain in position. They snaked around the towers and pillars in a sort of death grip that struck Jane as steadying, as well as suffocating. Some of the vines appeared to have pieces of bark missing, exposing an off-white colour beneath.

As they neared the house the tick of the clock became more prevalent, a booming chime accompanied by the sensation that the ground underneath them and the car rocked in unison with the clock. She hoped that neither her bedroom nor Mr Smithson's would be too close. Mr Whiteley pulled up and stopped the old car, it seemed to screech in protest before the large front doors. By the time she had carefully got out of the car, peeling the back of her legs from the leather, Mr Whiteley had removed her suitcase and was getting back into the car again.

'Goodbye Miss Elliot, I hope you find Hacket House to your liking,' Mr Whitely said, a peculiar expression on his now thin lips. Without allowing Jane chance to reply, the car drove away.

'Goodbye then Mr Whiteley,' Jane called, shaking her head as she watched the car roar away, leaving her standing before the large doors waving at the rapidly moving vehicle like an idiot.

'Miss Jane Elliot, I presume?'

With a small start, Jane spun around to face the front door where the voice seemed to have come from. One of the double doors was now open and a young woman, tall and bony with rod-straight red hair stood, illuminated by a light from within the house. She was wearing a smart pair of trousers and a shirt.

She could be a supermodel, thought Jane as she worked her own mouth into a smile and ascended the couple of steps. She no longer felt overdressed, and as the woman looked her up and down she was glad she had worn her best clothes.

'Yes hello, I'm Jane. You must be Miss Clarissa Lewis?'

Clarissa returned Jane's smile and stretched out her hand for Jane to take. It was like shaking the hand of a skeleton.

'Yes, although you may call me Clarissa.'

The two women made small talk as Clarissa led the way through the giant doorway and into the equally giant foyer of the house.

'Oh my, does someone collect clocks here?' Jane asked, looking around the deep rich red wooden space. Every surface had a ticking clock either on it or built into it. Not to mention the rows of different crooked and giant grandfather clocks that stood together on each side of the double staircase. It appeared that a number of doors had been squeezed between the variety of looming clocks. Jane suddenly realised they were also built into the sculpted staircases. The hum of the clocks lingered in the air like the buzzing of insects.

'Yes, Mr Smithson spent his life travelling the world collecting clocks and watches of all shapes and sizes. Then he employed a master clockmaker and learnt to build his own. That was it then, he sold his entire collection and rebuilt it all with his bare hands, using wood from this estate. He was particularly fond and proud of his grandfather clocks. He had the interior of the house gutted and remodelled to better suit his collection.' Clarissa's eyes gleamed in the dim light.

'Oh wow, he must have been very talented.... and very fond of ticking clocks?'

'Oh yes, Mr Smithson found the ticking of clocks like soothing music and I have to say that I agree. Their ticking masks the hum of the generator downstairs which Mr Smithson always hated, and the house has been managed in such a way that the clocks are never silent. But you'll get used to them just like I did when I first came here. Soon you'll find that you won't be able to sleep without the ticking of a clock beside you. But leave your case here and we'll go up so I can introduce you to Mr Smithson before dinner.'

With that, Clarissa glided towards and up the righthand staircase with Jane hurrying to keep up. On the walls, instead of portraits, were ticking clock faces in frames. Cracked and faded with age, their blank faces somehow gave more of an impression of observation than eyes. Some looked like they had been inserted into portraits or landscapes, but Jane had no time to examine them as she hurried after Clarissa. Jane followed Clarissa down deep red corridors, illuminated by dim glass light fittings and around sharp bends that seemed to run at right angles from one another. Like downstairs, every piece of furniture, every mirror and chair, contained a clock, upon every table there sat at least one clock. Guarding the corridor and on ever present watch were the tall twisted grandfather clocks that Jane had seen downstairs. Jane wondered if they had been built to fit the tall halls or if the tall halls had been built to accommodate the clocks. Jane suspected the later.

They walked to the end of a long corridor and stopped suddenly before a deep red door that was like all the others she had passed. Loomed over by a grandfather clock at each side, it was comprised of the same deep wood that camouflaged it against the rest of the corridor.

'This is Mr Smithson's room. Number 555. Five was his lucky number.' Clarissa pointed to a small brass number discretely placed beside the door.

'Are all the rooms numbered?'

'Oh yes, Mr Smithson had a great fondness for numbers.'

With that, Clarissa's hand seized the doorknob and the door swung open into a large, dimly lit chamber.

'After you,' Clarissa gestured, and Jane, with a renewed tingling of nerves, hesitated. She could smell something; she couldn't put her finger on it, but it was an irritant. She could still back out, Mr Whiteley could always take her back to the station and she could go anywhere, far from here. Living on the money she'd been saving and the bonus, she reckoned she could last six months if she looked after it. Spend all her time indoors hiding, terrified he would find her. Then she'd have to face both him and the past. And if he didn't find her and the world did not end, then what? She'd have to get a job and start saving again, put off her exile abroad another few years. Not to mention forfeit the pile of cash she had been offered to look after Mr Smithson. With a deep breath, thinking of walking tall along golden beaches on the other side of the world and having the freedom to explore them, a million miles from him, Jane stepped into the room.

One foot in front of the other, Jane approached the nursing bed. She could see it was the latest in nursing bed technology - she should have expected as much. The humming of the air mattress mingled with the ticking of the clocks as she looked down at the skinny, emaciated man lying on his side, his legs contracted in a permanent bend, his fingers contracted into permanent claws. She could tell he was alive by the rise and fall of his chest. She knew from what Clarissa had sent her that he couldn't speak, that there was very little that remained of the clock-building genius he had once been. At least he looked light and like he would be relatively easy to move. Along the walls surrounding the bed and looming over the sleeping man were eight grandfather clocks, each one taller than Jane. Their faces all faced inwards, their postures, each unique, gave them a much more human appearance than any clock had a right to have. It was like Mr Smithson was surrounded by a group of eight, no seven men; one she felt sure was female. Jane had the mad notion that they were watching them and that they would be watching her care for the old man. It made no sense but deep down past logic, Jane felt that she was correct. Their ticking voices were as individual as their frames and they overwhelmed and overpowered the room, even with its dramatic long velvet drapes and giant windows. Jane couldn't help wondering if the presence of the clocks was really what the current Mr Smithson would want if he could speak for himself. Stepping closer to the bed, Jane realised that the smell emanated from the man and she'd have to give him a very thorough wash tomorrow.

'Mr Smithson has dementia and sometimes wails in the night. Don't let it bother you. Nothing but strong medication can please or quiet him and Mr Smithson, when he was of sound mind and body, had legal documents drawn up that made it clear he did not want to receive medical intervention,' Clarissa said, looking down at Mr Smithson, her expression blank and reserved.

'He needs repositioning four-hourly day and night. In a nursing home, as you probably know, this would require two people, however he is light enough to be effectively cared for by one skilled carer. Should he need to go up the bed my colleague Dora, who you'll meet tonight, will assist you. His incontinence pads are to be changed when he is wet or soiled. He needs to be assisted to eat and drink, a minimum of 1400 ml a day if he will drink it, and he is to receive a body wash in the morning and a bath ideally once a week. I will arrange a home carer to come and assist with that as frequently as possible. The bathroom is just through here.' Clarissa crossed the room and opened a door Jane hadn't seen. For the first time she noticed the ceiling hoist that would carry Mr Smithson from the main bedroom and over to the boat-like high tech bath Jane knew would lift and lower at the push of a button. The white bath sink and toilet stood out stark against the rich red walls and four more large, looming clocks. Returning to the main bedroom they once again looked down upon the still silent Mr Smithson.

'Well Jane, are your duties acceptable?' Clarissa asked as if it wasn't too late for Jane to back out.

Surprised, Jane looked down at the man whose eyes were closed, the only sign that he was alive was the slow, rhythmic, barely visible rise and fall of his rib cage. He reminded her of pictures she'd seen of famine victims.

'Yes, what time do I start?'

Chapter 4

After she had turned Mr Smithson and offered him a drink from a child's beaker, Clarissa led Jane back down the wooden corridor. Her room was the second on the right, two doors away from Mr Smithson. Clarissa unlocked the door with a large brass key, which she gave to Jane along with a bunch of other keys.

'These should be all the keys you need for both the internal and external doors and gates.'

The door swung smoothly open, revealing a clean room with wood panelled walls. It was smaller than Mr Smithson's chamber, but big enough for a comfortable looking four-poster double bed hung with velvet curtains, a fat looking couch, and a deep red desk and wardrobes. Thick books lined the shelves and to Jane's relief there was only one clock, a large, twisted, bone-white tower on the mantelpiece that emitted a smooth tick every second. Sat on the red velvet bed throw was Jane's suitcase. Looking around the room, Jane smiled, it was by far the nicest room she'd ever had, and she'd wanted a four-poster bed ever since she was a girl. She'd never get closer to her fantasy than this room.

'Your time between caring for Mr Smithson is your own. Hacket House does not contain any televisions or radios, we have internet for any laptops or other devices you wish to use. You will find the password on the mantelpiece beside the clock. Please don't hesitate to ask either me or Dora for assistance. Dinner is at 7.30, just head downstairs and we will be in the first room on the right. I will leave you to prepare.'

Before Jane could ask anything else, Clarissa had swept from the room, swinging the door shut behind her. Jane got the distinct impression that Clarissa was extremely busy and wanted to get back to whatever other tasks she had to do.

It was only 7pm, so Jane set about unpacking her little suitcase and stowing away her meagre belongings in the large wardrobe and drawers provided. It didn't take her long. Jane was pleased to open up an old record player and a separate case containing a decent collection of records. Looking through them she was thrilled to find the single of Jefferson Airplane's White Rabbit. Carefully, she selected the record and the room was filled with life. Singing along, she began to examine the bookshelves. She had been expecting a load of musty classical books. She was pleasantly surprised to find that the leather-bound volumes, as well as containing some of her classical favourites, also contained modern murder mysteries and cosy mysteries. These were the only kind of books she'd read in years, she must have told Clarissa or Dora over the phone. She didn't remember telling them, or even Clarissa asking, but she must have at some point, surely. Selecting a book, she sat on the fat sofa that matched the bed spread, sinking into its loving embrace. Only to realise, after reading a couple of pages, that it was 7.25 and she had to head downstairs to dinner.

She was panting and slightly late by the time she reached the dining room, having taken a number of wrong turns and found a surprising number of sitting rooms and music rooms that all appeared to be unused but still not reprieved from the clock menace. In the dining room she found Clarissa and a large plump lady with a grey perm whom Clarissa introduced as Dora, the lady who helped with the cooking and upkeep of the house. The large woman whom Jane assessed as well over six feet tall beamed at her as if Jane was the answer to her prayers. Taking her hand and pumping it firmly up and down, Dora enquired about her journey, how far she'd come, how she liked the house, and what her favourite dessert was all in the same breath. Jane did her best to answer although her speech could never match the speed of her new friend.

'Jane why don't you sit next to Atticus?' Clarissa came to her rescue as Dora let out a whoop at the mention of strawberry tart. As the excited woman skipped into the kitchen, Jane took the seat at the table beside

Atticus who stood up and pulled the chair out for her. After his hurry to get away from the house, Jane was surprised to find him inside it. She thanked Atticus and sat down, looking at her companions, both of whom Jane noticed looked quietly pleased with themselves. Their expressions seemed far happier and far less tense than they were a mere half an hour ago. Jane wondered if there might be something going on between the pair.

Humming to herself, Dora bustled through and set a plate and cutlery onto the bare place mat in front of Jane. As she helped herself to the cheese and onion pie Atticus offered her, she wondered why it had not been set in advance. After all, they'd known she was coming. The homemade food, after months of either her own cooking or ready meals, tasted divine. Dora quivered in her seat when Jane complimented it.

'All meals are like this you know, we don't go for that premade junk here,' Dora beamed, helping herself to a large piece of meat pie. Clarissa asked if the room was satisfactory, and Jane affirmed that she was delighted with it. Atticus alone remained silent as he ate his meal beside her, emitting a quiet warmth Jane was certain had not been present earlier. After a dessert of Bakewell tart and cream, Dora promised that tomorrow's dessert would be a pleasant surprise, as Jane helped take the empty plates into the kitchen.

'After dinner we sit in the snug just off the dining room.' Dora said as they left the dishes by the sink. Dora led the way back to the now empty dining room and through a side door into a well-lit lounge with comfy chairs, overflowing bookshelves, and a table beside the window where Atticus sat. The table in front of him was covered in jigsaw pieces. Clarissa sat curled up on a fat sofa in front of the fire, flicking through a magazine. She looked up and smiled as they entered the room. Jane looked at the clock over the fire and found that it was just before nine.

'Ah Jane, would you care to help me complete my puzzle?' Atticus asked, a pair of glasses balanced upon his nose.

'Yes ok,' Jane found herself smiling as she joined Atticus. As they worked together in a contented silence, Dora continued to hum as she sat knitting what looked suspiciously like one of the blankets she had seen on Mr Smithson's bed. She was sure she recognised the tune, but their silent companionship was so content that she didn't wish to break it.

At ten o'clock, Jane wished her companions goodnight and went upstairs to Mr Smithson, whom she cleaned, changed, then turned, before offering him an Ensure supplement. The same smell as earlier still assaulted her nostrils but in her career she had smelt far, far worse.

Going back to her room and locking the door, she changed into her pyjamas as the excitement of the day suddenly turned to tiredness. Jane slipped under the rich cotton sheets and seemed to sink into the mattress as if it embraced her. As sleep seduced her into its warm depths, the tune Dora had hummed seemed to follow her down the rabbit hole and Jane remembered what it was just before the world went black. It was the immortal White Rabbit by Jefferson Airplane.

Chapter 5

Jane's alarm woke her at two and again at six, when, half asleep, she went to tend to Mr Smithson. Having no capacity to understand his disturbance, the old man cried out and Jane sympathised as she woke him up yet again before heading back to her own bed. After the six o'clock turn and change she could not go back to sleep, instead lying in bed and reading her book until seven when she rose and dressed in her comfortable day clothes.

She had three more hours until she was due to care for Mr Smithson. How was she going to distract herself until then? Maybe she could see what else her new home had to offer? She went down endless deep wooden corridors, each one looked almost identical except with clocks in slightly different places. Every single one of them was an individual, like the clocks in Mr Smithson's room, as if she was walking down a street of people instead of a deserted corridor. She went through every open door and found mostly decent sized rooms like her own, with rich fat furniture and more clocks that beat a tattoo which followed her journey through the house as if she was in a film rather than a real house. She found a library full of leather-bound books in foreign languages, classical literature, and locked cabinets. In every room she examined the clocks, some seemed friendly, she wasn't sure why, others contained an air of menace so great she could hardly bare to look at them. Some seemed almost human whilst others felt like frozen predators waiting to pounce and tear her apart. Others she found her hands caressing as if they were old friends or pets, one which she found in a deserted bedroom she found herself holding like a long-lost love before coming to her senses, leaping backwards and almost dropping the lean tall *muscular* thing. Shaking her head and wondering if she had been single for far too long, Jane hurried from the room. She found her way downstairs into the large kitchen, clearly designed to feed a vast household and comprised, like the rest of the house, of rich wood, in this case polished and varnished until it achieved a mirror-like sheen. The giant cast iron range appeared like a crouching bear in the grass. Her stomach rumbling and, ignoring the cereal and bread Dora had left out, she scoured the kitchen and cooked herself a simple breakfast of poached eggs and smoked salmon. She was relieved to find a microwave behind one of the red mirrors. She sat and ate at the large wooden table under the gaze of a particularly vicious looking old clock with cleaving knives for hands and hammer-like weights on chains which Jane hadn't noticed the previous evening. She then washed up her things before heading out of a door that led neither to the dining room nor where she had been and found herself in the main entrance hall.

Jane jumped backwards with a start, suddenly wishing that she'd eaten less. Standing directly in front of her, half hidden in the shadows and staring at her, was a young sever woman wearing something black that blended her into the shadows, giving the disturbing impression that her head was suspended in thin air. Her straw-coloured hair stuck out in every direction like a crown of thorns, her dark eyes stared at Jane, her cracked lips were twisted in a scowl. The woman did not smile or say anything as they stared at one another and Jane's heart thumped in her chest. The woman was so pale Jane wouldn't be surprised to learn that she was a ghost, but Atticus was right, ghosts didn't exist except in your mind. But all words were lost to her. If her life depended upon it, she wouldn't have been able to utter a peep.

Without warning, the woman spun away and disappeared into the gloom of the corner. After a few aching seconds, Jane crossed over to find only a blank wall and a cold breeze where the woman had disappeared. Jane turned and ran up the main stairs as fast as her legs would take her, and before she knew it she found herself in Mr Smithson's tomb. Soggy Weetabix and a beaker of juice sat on the bedside table waiting for her. She picked up the Weetabix and found it to be still warm. She fed him the sloppy, sweet mess and wiped his mouth, before giving him the best wash she could manage with lots of soap and changing his soiled pad before giving him the juice. All the while, the giant clocks loomed over them like ghostly figures, especially ghostly in the bedsheets Jane had draped over their faces. She'd started doing it in the night whilst half asleep, but it had seemed like the right thing to do, to prevent these strangers from looking at her sweat and toil and Mr Smithson's flesh. She knew it was crazy and God knows what Clarissa would say, but it felt right somewhere deep in her marrow. She'd just have to remember to remove the sheets when she was done this time.

Despite washing every inch of skin she could get to, changing the bedding and the man's loose t-shirt, the stench remained. The strong chemical smell of Lavender slowly, sip by sip, was replaced by the putrid stench of the man in the bed. It was stronger than before, as if the smell was determined not to be covered. Something else troubled Jane as she became more and more reluctant to lean forwards with the cup. It was not how he looked or smelt, she had seen plenty of emaciated, contracted old people in beds, smelled more shit, sweat and piss than she cared to admit to anyone. No, there was something disgusting about this man, but she couldn't put her finger on what exactly as he slurped up his thickened juice. Whilst the clocks, now uncovered, looked down on them both, somehow their numbered faces were worse than eyes. At least eyes indicated life and could close. Hinted that there was some commonality between the watcher and the watched, Jane shuddered under their cold gazes, and as soon as Mr Smithson refused to drink any more, she hurried from the room, slamming the door shut behind her.

That night at dinner, after her second glass of wine, Jane asked about the woman in the black dress.

'There is nobody else in the house Jane,' Clarissa smiled.

'Yes dear, it's just the five of us, you must have seen a reflection of yourself,' Dora chimed in. An awkward silence followed, only broken by the ticking of the clocks that surrounded them. Dora's round cheeks flushed a deeper red. Jane fought the urge to laugh at the white peoples' discomfort. Being part Jamaican, her skin was a good deal darker than the woman she'd seen, her hair was also far too dark to ever be confused for blonde. They all knew that she couldn't possibly be the anaemic looking pale woman with yellow hair.

'You must have seen a ghost then Jane,' broke in Atticus, as if he could not stand the silence any longer. 'It might have been the wife. If you see her again, tell her I miss her boot print on my arse.'

Atticus smiled as if he was joking, but Jane knew he wasn't and that the woman had not been his wife.

'Would you like to help me complete London Bridge Jane? I have new glasses and I'm feeling hot tonight.'

'You'd do better with a magnifying glass,' Jane smiled, allowing the atmosphere to shatter as she got up from the table.

Chapter 6

Jane's second night was a rough one. She tossed and turned in her large bed, unable to sleep as the sound of the clocks passed through her and her own unpleasant thoughts and memories haunted her. First, she wondered about the woman, she had looked far too solid to be a ghost, and why her companions would lie about the presence of another resident of Hacket House. Such thoughts were chased away by memories of him and Rowena, the sounds of her own screams eventually lulling her to sleep just as the alarm on her phone went off, telling her it was time to turn Mr Smithson again. The pattern continued throughout the night; she'd wake to turn him, his room so oppressive she could barely remain in there, then go back to bed and struggle to sleep again. Then, when she'd finally dropped off, in no time at all she would have to be up again turning the old body. At six am as she stumbled down the corridor after the last night turn, her tired mind telling her that someone was at the opposite end of the corridor, concealed behind a clock. Maybe it was that woman? Jane was too tired to care or wonder whether or not she was imagining it.

A few hours later at around ten, Jane got up to wash, feed and change Mr Smithson, then she removed the bedsheets. She told herself that she must have imagined the figure, that it was only the long shadow of a clock. After her own breakfast, Jane went and explored the downstairs of the house, trying to find the prettier rooms and windows Dora had insisted the house possessed last night over the Cumberland sausages and mash. Atticus had rolled his eyes over his mash and Jane was keen to see who was right. After a thorough exploration, Jane concluded that she had to agree with Atticus. There was little of any beauty about the house, just more elaborate clocks. The exception was the muscular clock, which reminded her of Patrick Bateman's body and felt smooth under her dry hands. Towering over her as if leaning in for a kiss, its clock face, pretty much like all the others, somehow felt warm and inviting as it observed her and Jane was alarmed to find herself murmuring up at the thing under its hot gaze. Shaking her head, Jane told herself she just needed more sleep and hurried out from under its smouldering gaze.

In another room she bumped into the woman in the black dress again, standing before a mantelpiece and staring up at a clock with about ten identical clock faces. What appeared to be an old carpet beater was clutched in her white hands. Her nails were bare and overgrown and looked far more like claws than nails. The woman did nothing to acknowledge Jane's presence and ignored her greeting. In fact, she didn't move, only the rise and fall of her chest, rapid as if she had just come running, was the only thing that told Jane the woman wasn't a statue. In the better light Jane was able to see that the black robe was in fact a Victorian style concoction of hoops and many skirts. She dared not move close enough to see the woman's face that was covered by the matted straw hair that hung over it. Finally, Jane was able to drag herself away from the woman and headed down another corridor, finding herself at a back door leading into the garden.

It was a bright but cool day and the garden was a brilliant arsenic green, beautiful and wild like The Secret Garden. It had been one of her favourite stories, but she'd burnt it along with the Harry Potter's and other large sections of her book collection. She wandered through the twisted maze of trees, plants and jewel-like wildflowers. The songs of birds and the cries of animals she did not recognise were a welcome relief from the strange woman, echoing clocks, and Mr Smithson's dementia rattles. She found the remains of a stone path, broken up and destroyed by the growth of weeds and the roots of the twisted trees. She found painted wooden statues, almost totally consumed by the ivy and toppling to the sides on their slab bases. The ground was rutted and muddy and her inadequate boots slid in the mud, but outside in the sun, she was happier than she had been in months. Behind a dense patch of bushes, Jane stumbled into a large granite fountain. Using the cold slimy granite to get her balance, she noticed the crack in the stone that allowed the still miraculously flowing fountain to trickle out and flood the garden. Mallard ducks and moorhens paddled, squawked and waded in the remains. How had she not heard them before? Jane threw back her head and laughed, startling the fowls that squawked back and flapped their wings. It was the best and most chaotic garden she had ever seen.

Reluctantly, the clock pierced Jane's peace, telling her that it was yet again time to enter the dreary house and turn the decrepit creature in the bed. As soon as she'd done that, she'd fed him the liquidized mess of meat and mash under the gaze of the clocks. She hadn't bothered with the sheets, all it did was prolong her time in the oppressive room. Besides, the clocks felt less intrusive now that Atticus had moved them back against the walls of the chamber. Jane returned to the garden with her own late lunch. After lunch, finding that it was only three pm, Jane decided to walk down to the little village of Bramley that Clarissa and Dora had talked about. Atticus had been less enthusiastic about the place, describing it as a dead-end place with nothing but a decent pub. Jane wanted to be outside the shadow of the house and judge the place for herself.

After some searching, Jane found a pedestrian gate inserted into a thick hedge at the edge of the property. It was a construction of intricate iron swirls just like the main gate, but it was also locked, so Jane fished her set of keys from out of her pocket. The third one fitted, and with a metallic screech the key turned and Jane was out on the pathless country road. Running down the hill towards the little cottages, Jane was stunned by the sound of her own laughter, but she couldn't stop. Self-consciously, she slowed to a walk as she approached the nearest cottage.

It was ancient stone, lopsided in places with a chipped granite roof. The other cottages she came across, sitting haphazardly in wonky straightish lines, were similar. Comprised of old granite or dark old brick with low windows and doors, some had thatched roofs instead of slate but still sat grey with age. Others had red instead of brown doors; they all looked similar with only minor differences. Nothing was younger than a hundred years and there wasn't a barn conversion in sight. The only modern touch seemed to be the too many cars that fought for space down the narrow streets. Otherwise it could have been 1900 and something. Walking down long winding streets and alleys, every person she came across smiled and said hello as they passed her. Some people even waved at her from their houses and Jane tried to smile back at them. The people she saw were of all ages, but all appeared to be white which wasn't that uncommon. But in no village or town she had ever been to had the residents been so eager to greet her. Jane told herself nothing was wrong as a group of teenage boys in school uniform yelled 'Hello Jane' from across the street and, wishing they'd leave her alone, she waved back.

She found what felt like the centre of the village and, parked beside a crossroads with a war memorial erected in the centre, sat a deserted children's playground. It was much larger and more impressive than Jane would have thought such a small village warranted, with its high slides, vibrant climbing frame, and matching swings which would allow the children to soar over the garden of headstones next door. It seemed in rather poor taste. The graves were undoubtedly older than the park which was the most modern structure she had seen in the village so far. She wondered if a church had once sat beside the graveyard, it struck her as fairly likely. But who the hell demolishes a church and replaces it with a garish playground? Peering around the park from the safety of the bright red fence, she had no desire to get any closer. Jane looked for signs of a structure or the foundations of a building. There was no sign she could see that a building had ever existed there. Jane had wanted to get married in a church, not because she was religious, but because that was where people in her family got married. He'd talked her out of it, said they'd save up and do the big wedding after the baby was born. They'd ended up in a basic little registry office, hardly the grand affair of Jane's dreams, nor meeting her families wishes. Jane's eyes burned as she spun away, leaving the playground with its garden of the dead.

She found a few shops, an ancient post office, an even older pub with a sign saying it dated back to the reformation, a butchers with its dead window display, a greengrocers, a library, and other little shops, the type that are dying out on most high streets, but seemed to be thriving in Bramley. The people in the shops grinned as they waved at her too and Jane thought they seemed similar to one another, but she couldn't put her finger on why. Jane guessed that the locals hadn't discovered the joys of the outside world of supermarkets and online shopping yet. Strangest of all were the people she saw staring at her, fixed grins on their faces after they'd greeted her. Some greeted her then whispered together, one old man muttered 'Afternoon Miss Elliot,' before crossing himself and scuttling headfirst into the pub. Jane didn't mind, they were clearly not used to outsiders, and besides, what were a few stares and some superstitious nonsense? Clarissa said they discouraged strangers and Jane could easily believe it. They must know that she had come from Hacket House, that was all. They'd soon get used to her.

Tempted by the aroma of fresh bread and pastries, Jane ducked into a small bakery with little tables displaying bread, pastries and cakes on piled high trays; there was no modern glass counter. She ordered a glass of homemade lemonade and a cake from a middle-aged woman who grinned at her like a Cheshire cat, then sat at a little table. She was the only customer in the café and, looking at her phone, she saw it was just gone four. Too late for the lunchtime crowd, Jane figured, as she pulled her book from her bag and began to read.

'Hi, you must be new here?' Jane jumped at the high-pitched voice and looked up to see a woman, close to her own age with a big smile and blond curly hair.

'Did I startle you? I'm sorry, I'm always startling mum at home. I move so quietly, then talk so loudly she swears I'm a ghost. I'm Molly by the way.'

'I'm Jane, it's ok, I was just reading. And yes, I only came yesterday.'

'Ah, can I sit here?'

'Erm yeah, sure,' replied Jane, moving her coat and bag.

As they ate their food and drank their drinks the two women talked. Well, it was mainly Molly who did most of the talking and that suited Jane. She leant that Molly was thirty, slightly older than she'd guessed, that she lived at home with her mum and dad because she couldn't afford to move out anywhere decent in the village on the wages she earned being a hairdresser at the local salon. She laughed at the appropriate places when Molly told her about the villagers and their peculiar habits and secrets. Then, when it seemed appropriate and before Molly could start describing the local police officer Mr Hubbs' on-duty sleeping habits, Jane asked Molly about the house and its inhabitants.

For the first time since they'd met Molly was silent as she studied Jane, clearly eager to share her knowledge but also calculating just how much she should share.

'You know it's meant to be haunted, don't you?' Molly said at last, taking a long sip of tea.

'So Atticus told me.'

'Yeah he's is a strange one, Lying Whiteley the kids call him.'

'Why?' Jane frowned.

'Oh, just rumours that's all, you know his wife died under suspicious circumstances, don't you?'

'She fell, didn't she?'

'That's what the police said, couldn't prove anything otherwise even though everyone here knew they hated each other. Some people still think he caved her head in and them up at the house covered for him.' Molly grinned as Jane shuddered.

'Not many people would live that close to Hacket House, especial not on the same land and definitely not for anywhere near as long as he has been there.'

'How long has he been there?'

'Twenty years. His wife was this crazy bitch from a village a few miles away and she made him move on site. He was already maintenance man and gardener. He knew Mr Smithson before he went mad. Dora has been there fifteen, Mad Dolly's been there ten years and Clarissa four years. No one else has stayed longer than five months. None of poor Mr Smithson's carers, none of the maids, no one else can stand being in that house or on that land any longer.'

'Who is 'Mad Dolly'?' Jane snapped. 'What do you mean 'went mad'? He has dementia, he hasn't gone mad!'

'Some relative of Dora's who can't go out and haunts the house like a ghost. You're probably right. It was probably just the dementia setting in. It started about fifteen years ago, soon after Dora came, bad luck for her but she braved it all with nothing more than the odd belt of whiskey; the restlessness, he'd run around that house for days and days, sometimes all he'd do was build his clocks, rambling to himself, screaming at all hours of the day and night. It wasn't until he tried to strangle Dora one morning, when she came into his room with breakfast on a tray, that they sent him off for assessment. They diagnosed dementia but my Mam, who was his first carer after he was released home and doped up, wanted to get the place exorcised. There'd been rumours the place was haunted since she was a girl, stories of ghosts roaming around the place. One of them being some crack pot old demon worshiper, his ghost is meant to be blacker than the deepest hole, but she never saw him. One of the maids, a mouthy woman from Zimbabwe reckoned she saw it, right in Mr Smithson's room, and she left that day just after she told my Ma and just vanished from the village. Ma thought that one of them had driven him mad and that maybe one had possessed him. She lasted about a month before jacking it in after she'd woken up one night during a sleep-in to find him stood over her bed howling his head off like the Goddamn Joker. She hasn't worked since and still has nightmares. Have you seen anything strange?'

'No,' Jane said, trying to keep her voice normal as a growing coldness crept through her veins. 'Is Atticus still the gardener? It's in a right state now.'

Molly suddenly became very interested in cutting up her gingerbread man.

'Yeah well, gardens have a mind of their own and he's probably kept busy maintaining all them clocks and the giant generators.' That made perfect sense to Jane, as Molly selected the gingerbread man's head and took a bite.

'Do you know Clarissa?' Jane asked as Molly chewed and swallowed. She shook her head.

'No not really, once in a blue moon Whiteley will take her to town. My Ma reckons she's a distant relative of Mr Smithson or something. Damn their gingerbread is good, it's Caroline's secret recipe. Do you want to try a leg?'

Thoughtfully Jane took the offered leg, it was just as good as Molly said. Molly talked about her ambition to become a dog groomer and to one day have her work displayed at Crufts. After they had finished they went to the little library, just before it closed, and Jane opened an account despite her dismay at the oversized romance section. The librarian, Donald, directed her to the crime section whilst Molly mooned over the paranormal romances. She was relieved to find that it was a reasonable size and had a number of books that caught her interest. They chose their books then headed out.

'I'll give you a lift up to the gates if you like,' Molly offered, bemused as Jane struggled with the first few Harry Potter books.

'That would be a great help thanks,' Jane smiled. Sat in Molly's Ford KA with the radio blaring as Molly hurtled at high speed down country roads, Jane gripped her books tightly, almost wishing she'd walked and wondered if there was something in the water supply that made the locals drive as if they had a death wish.

Chapter 7

It started to rain just as Molly pulled up and, carrying her new books, Jane hurried along the cracked drive to the house. Molly had refused to get any closer to the house, even after Jane had unlocked the gate. With a shudder, she claimed that the place gave her the 'heebee jeebees', big time. After what Jane had heard, it didn't surprise her. They had however arranged to go for a long walk in the surrounding countryside on Jane's Saturday off. She and Richard had enjoyed going for hikes together, the thought was out before she could stop it and she flinched, pushing it down under its slab where it belonged. The house loomed closer and closer and Jane watched it close in on her, focusing on every wood stain, ever pillar, every exposed white bone of the ivy and the ticking of the clock with its moving second hand. She saw it reach 5.30 and felt the boom of the tick just as a black shadow, long and thin stepped across the clock face and stepped under the shadowed overhang of the roof in two long strides. Jane stopped and stared for a second, mouth open in an O shape. Then she shook her head and sighed, she just needed a good night's sleep, that was all. Clutching the books tightly, she hurried into the house and up the stairs to her room where she piled them on the table. She'd start the first book after dinner.

This time caring for Mr Smithson was far harder. As she touched him with her rubber-gloved hand, Mr Smithson's toothless mouth opened and unleashed a hellish rattle of such volume that Jane felt her ears ache. She would never have guessed it was made by a human and was far worse than any of the other dementia rattles she had heard previously. It caused her to shudder, making the hair on the back of her neck stand up on end. It was like some large animal was being tortured, the shock of it causing her to almost drop his permanently bent legs back onto the airflow mattress. Jane kept hold though and gritted her teeth, ignoring the tortured ever-screaming face as it stared up in her direction, his arms contracted against the side of his chest. His hands forced into permanent claws, which needed pads to stop his nails piercing his flesh, could not move to fight her or whatever his bulging eyes saw when they stared up in her direction. He could not fight her, but his body became stiffer than normal, forcing her to apply more pressure to open his hands and knees. Sweating as a mixture of pity and frustration washed over her, she pushed the slide sheet under him and used it to move him to the opposite side of the mattress and laid him on his other side. Mr Smithson's howls increased as she used a small amount of force to prise his legs open enough to remove the incontinence pad that was constantly wedged in place, keeping him as dry as possible. The man continued to scream as she removed her rubber gloves and the wet pad and returned to him, attempting to give him a drink and his warm, liquidised meal which he greedily took, seeming to forget about whatever had caused the hellish screams in the first place. As he lapped up the thickened sludge of juice, Jane silently cursed the foolish men, she was convinced they'd have to be men, who'd decided that staying alive no matter the cost was a scientific endeavourer worth pursuing. Looking down at the pitiful excuse of a human being before her she shuddered again. As the drink was finished and she was writing up the chart, the dementia rattle began again. Unable to bear any more noise, Jane left without looking back. Experience told her that nothing she could say would make a difference and that there was nothing more she could do for him.

Jane wandered the corridors and the crazy staircases with their mystical angles as the howls tore through the house and seemingly though her mind. Jane was so tired that she could barely keep her eyes open. No wonder she was starting to see things. She'd read about carers in America, illegal immigrants held as slaves who were forced to look after multiple old people with no spare time, fuck all sleep and their wages withheld. Jane's blurred mind wondered if she would get paid the proper amount, part of her now deeply regretted moving away from her previous agency. Thank goodness she would be paid weekly, she thought, wondering how none of the imprisoned immigrants seemed to have ended up murdering the more annoying or pitiful of their charges. Maybe they did. Who would look too closely if someone expected to die soon, shock horror, dropped dead one day? She could see it happening more than anyone who'd never cared for an awkward person would ever dare admit. She wondered if she would ever murder Mr Smithson; it may well become a viable option if he kept screaming like this. It was enough to drive anyone mad, though it didn't seem to have driven Clarissa mad, the jury was still out on Dora. Clarissa seemed to Jane to be the kind of woman who had a cast iron constitution. No, it would take a lot to get under Clarissa's skin, even if Mr Smithson was a relative.

Jane was surprised to find herself back in her bedroom, not entirely remembering how she got there. Collapsing onto her covers, she was asleep in seconds despite Mr Smithson's wails, which she could still hear even in her dreams. Before she knew it, the alarm was going off at ten o'clock, again it was time for Jane to get up and turn and feed the man in the bed.

In modern day care, you're not supposed to say feed, your meant to say assist even if there is nothing they can do except open their toothless black holes to accept the spoon with the liquidised gunk. Clearly a term developed by some care professional who'd never dealt with a shitty pad, Jane thought as she stumbled down the corridor, too preoccupied with her own internal ramblings to notice that the wailing had stopped.

Soon she was back in bed and feeling better, eating the cheese sandwiches Dora had thoughtfully left beside her door along with a note saying they understood about Jane missing dinner, that her body clock would readjust in a couple of days, and that they looked forward to seeing her tomorrow. She'd have to find Dora in the morning and thank her. After she ate, she finished the book she had been reading. The poodle identified the murderer, a slightly strange outsider in the pretty little candy cane village, and the pretty, slightly ditzy, amateur sleuth shared a kiss with the ruggedly handsome and determined police officer who'd spent the book telling her not to interfere, then saving her from the murderer. Nothing like cute pets, a few murders and a happy ending. Jane knew they were cheesier than her sandwiches, but she couldn't get enough of them. Wishing she'd married a ruggedly handsome noble hero of a police officer instead of Richard, and lived in a cookie cutter village with at least one dog instead of a haunted house with a dementia patient and a woman no one would admit existed, Jane drifted off to sleep. Despite the promising start, it was another bad night, the clocks of the house ticked endlessly, disturbing her sleep. Then in the small hours of the morning, after the two am turn, Jane heard the creaking of the floorboards and the rushing of strange footsteps outside her door. She tossed and turned before losing her temper and storming out of bed. Flinging the door open and stepping into the corridor, its dim lights illuminating just enough to show that there was absolutely nobody out there, despite what she was certain she'd heard.

Chapter 8

After the six am turn, Jane gave up trying to sleep. Getting dressed into a comfortable pair of grey trousers and a soft top, she groggily made her way down the winding corridors and twisted staircases to the kitchen. The uneven floors creaked and wobbled so much in places that the ticking grandfather clocks rocked on their stands before stabilizing and meeting her gaze. They seemed to be daring her to rock them further, to give them an excuse to crash to the ground and crush her, so she slowed her pace. She was amazed they didn't wake up the entire household. After slightly longer than normal, and meeting nobody, she made it to the kitchen and began preparing herself breakfast. During the long night, she had resolved to find someone, Clarissa, Dora, the woman in the black dress, Atticus, any other member of staff who had evaded her and demand to know what the hell was happening throughout the night. Who the hell had been in Mr Smithson's room moving the damn clocks? They'd been so close to the bed that she'd barely been able get near it.

She had reasoned that the most likely place to pin down either Clarissa or Dora was in the kitchen. She ate her breakfast and waited, still nobody came and Jane wondered if she was the only one within the household. After all, she hadn't seen anybody but that woman, except at mealtimes. Maybe they didn't really work at the house, maybe they just rocked up at mealtimes to give her the impression that she was a part of a household of people.

At ten-ish, after Jane had returned from attempting to give Mr Smithson his breakfast, Clarissa swept through the kitchen, long red hair braided at the back and wearing a semi-transparent silk night dress that clung to her bones. A far too personal item, in Jane's opinion, to wear in a house where you and other people worked. She looked more like the lady of the house, a gold digger married to a decrepit husk of a man biding her time until he died, than a housekeeper. Maybe she even hoped that it would be Jane who relieved the old man's suffering. Clarissa, without looking at the table where Jane sat watching her, swept to the fridge and selected a carton of low-fat milk, closing the door before turning around. Jane saw the woman visibly jump, the milk diving from her long fingers and crashing to the floor where the plastic tub cracked.

'Jesus, why didn't you say anything? You almost made me jump out of my skin!' Clarissa gasped, her sharp white cheek bones reddening.

'Sorry, it was another long night and I was half asleep.' Jane's voice sounded half dead, even to her own ears.

'Well....' Jane could see Clarissa trying to regain her composure.

'How are you finding your time with us?' Clarissa binned the milk in a hidden bin and retrieved another, taking her seat at the wooden table opposite Jane.

'Ok, most of the time. I went into the village yesterday.'

'Oh, it's very pretty isn't it? I wish I had more time to go.'

'Yes, I met a woman in the village who said you hardly ever go down there.' Clarissa's cheekbones deepened and appeared to sharpen in the harsh light.

'I am afraid Jane, that this house and whoever occupies it have always been the subject of foolish gossip. I advise you to take no notice of it.' Clarissa smiled, but it was so forced it seemed to stretch the bottom half of her face.

'Oh, I'm used to gossip, I once lived with a lady, sweetest lady ever. The village she lived in decided that she deliberately poisoned her husband. They could see that she was struggling, going to the shops, then forgetting what she'd gone there for, forgetting her money or keys, forgetting people's names. No one helped her care for her disabled husband or herself. Then when her husband died after she'd cooked them both expired food, they turned on her like a pack of wolves. She was virtually a prisoner in her house, forever searching for her husband or children. Sometimes even her parents, by the time I moved in.'

'Well...quite.' Like most people she told about the difficult realities in the world of caring for old people, Clarissa didn't know what to say. Jane could see the discomfort in her face and smiled slightly.

'Was there some sort of party last night that I wasn't invited to?'

Clarissa looked up from her carton of milk.

'No, this house has not seen a party of any kind in over twenty years.'

'Then who were the people rushing past my bedroom all night, creaking the floorboards and rocking those priceless clocks?' Jane demanded, watching Clarissa closely. The other woman smiled.

'No one was in the house last night, other than me and Dora of course. Old houses creak in the night sometimes, that is all. It's nothing to worry about, the house is structurally sound.'

'This was not the natural creaking of an old house. This was a stampede of people going past all night.'

'I'm sorry Jane but you must have been asleep and dreaming. If there were such people in the house do you not think I would have heard or seen them? Not to mention let them in?'

'Didn't you?'

'No, I did not, it was just a dream because you are in a strange new house and that fool from the village probably put a lot of superstitious nonsense in your head.'

'Does it look like I slept to you?' Jane forced a smile, and she saw Clarissa hesitate.

'Well.... Not much, I admit, but Mr Smithson needs a lot of care.' Jane could see where the conversation was going and stood up.

'You are right, Mr Smithson does need a lot of care, as do a lot of other people. Oh, and by the way, speaking of care, I would warn whoever your visitors are to keep it down in future, or the village will have something new to gossip about. Oh, and tell them to watch the uneven floorboards and to leave the clocks where they are, we wouldn't want any of Mr Smithson's priceless clocks to go toppling over would we?'

Shaking with anger, Jane got up and stormed from the kitchen without another word. How dare that woman suggest to her, the queen of night turns and round the clock care, that a slight, non-violent man trapped in a bed was too much for her! How dare she suggest that his needs were greater than the fifty million other people who needed care! Still seething, Jane opened a creaky door and found herself in the clock-lined foyer of the house facing the front door.

'I'll go for a walk, I'll feel better when I'm out of this house.'

Stepping out, Jane found the morning to be cold and brisk, just the ticket to wake her up and send her into the front garden. She picked her way through the wilderness to the gate. It was an undeniable relief to be surrounded by birdsong instead of the ticking of clocks. Through the gate she set off at a brisk pace towards the village, planning to go to the bakery and have some lunch.

Without thought, Jane opened the door and stepped into the bakery. She stopped dead in her tracks, today the bakery was full. For the first time in years Jane found herself surrounded by smiling mums and their babies. They sat at ever rustic table with their coffees and cakes, they stood and laughed together blocking the shop's aisle and barring the way to the counter. Holding their babies or rocking prams, most of which were designer, she was disgusted to see, Jane felt as if she was about to cry. She felt as if these happy women were being deliberately cruel to her, forcing all the emptiness and grief to the surface. Staring at the chubby baby girl in the arms of the woman nearest to her, she wondered if she had been as selfish in her own happiness.

The baby was blonde with blue eyes, not as beautiful as her little Rowena, whose smile had lit up the room as well as melting everybody's hearts. Rowena had been chubby too, especially her little face, but her hair had been dark, her skin olive, her eyes like chocolate and Jane, who had always been allergic to pink had never forced the baby into pink monstrosities like the one this baby wore. Despite the baby's obvious difference and inferiority to her own Rowena, Jane knew that with half a chance she would snatch her up in her aching empty arms and take her away. She'd take the baby far from here and pretend it was hers, pretend that Rowena had never passed away before her second birthday. Protect this baby from any father, who needs a dad anyway? She'd join a mums group like this one, make friends, and Jane would become a selfishly contented bitch like the women around her and forget that babies ever died and left shattered shells behind.

'Do you want to get past?'

Jane ignored the woman's voice as she stared hungrily at the baby that looked curiously back up at her. The baby was lifted around out of Jane's eyesight and she tore her eyes away to look up at the anxious looking mother.

'Hey, are you ok?' the young woman's suspicion had turned to concern, and Jane realised that she was crying.

'You have a beautiful baby, look after her,' Jane managed to choke out before turning and fleeing from the shop. She heard the woman call after her but she kept running. Even if the woman wanted to chase after her, by the time she got the designer pram, Jane would be long gone. Rowena's had been designer, her father had insisted nothing was too good for his little princess.

The last thing she wanted was a confrontation with the woman or even worse, the woman prying. She carried on running, out of the village, she didn't care where too as long as she was away from the mothers group. It wasn't until she heard the chime of the clock in the distance that Jane realised she was in the depth of the house's garden. She ambled around for a few hours, climbing through the long, burnt-orange grass and gnarled red trees, into the most secluded spots. Jane wondered if she had made the right choice carrying on without Rowena, whether prolonging Rowena's existence in this world though her memory and working towards living out her dreams of paradise and taking Rowena was right. She didn't know if there was paradise after death, or if her own mum would be waiting there for her, Rowena in her arms. But she knew there was paradise on earth, she'd seen the pictures.

Behind a particularly giant and monstrous tree, Jane found a small rotten fence. Behind the black decay, just above the towering grass there appeared to be a number of moss-covered stones. The area in front of one of the stones looked less overgrown, its headstone looked newer and less covered in dark moss. Jane slowly followed the fence around, certain there had to be a gate into the little graveyard. After a while she spotted it, it matched the fence so completely that she could only tell it apart by the large padlock securing it shut. The only sound in the place was the distant thump of the clock and Jane looked at the little graveyard, wondering about Rowena's resting place. Had he found it yet? If she stayed at the house, hell even if she didn't, could she move it here? He'd never find it here, you couldn't even see it from the house, besides that tree guarded it. It was crazy but she knew it would never let the likes of him pass by, not on its watch. Jane started looking guiltily up at the tree that seemed to watch her. What the hell had made her think such a thing? It was just a tree. The alarm on her phone went off, half an hour until it was time to turn Mr Smithson. Reluctantly she turned from the tree and headed back in the direction she knew the house to be in. On the way to Mr Smithson's room, she stopped off at her own. Folded up on the bed was a note from Clarissa, informing her that Mr Smithson had been reassessed, that he wouldn't need care from eleven pm until six am. That night at dinner, Clarissa was polite as normal, neither her nor Jane mentioned the note nor their argument in the kitchen.

Chapter 9

The next few days passed by in a blur. A cycle of turns and the ticking of clocks, then dinner with the others where Dora would beam creepily at her, overly concerned and fussy about Jane and deliberately evasive about herself. She and Atticus would talk, play games or read as they grew more comfortable in each other's company. The nights passed by to the rhythm of footsteps, creeping past the more wobbly floorboards then hurrying where the floor was most solid. Combined with the creaking and humming of the old house it was as if the deserted place came alive at night. She had accepted the notes instructions with a great level of suspicion, she had never known that an assessment had taken place or ever known someone whose level of care apparently dropped so dramatically. Not, at least, when the patient was so well able to pay for it themselves. She suspected that Clarissa wanted her out of the way of whatever the nocturnal visitors were up to. A suspicion confirmed the next day when, over Jane's breakfast in the kitchen, Clarissa advised Jane that a larger room with a better view had been prepared for her at the front of the house. A whole floor would separate her from Mr Smithson. They had argued for some time on the subject until Jane, shaking and flushed with anger, stood up and declared that it was clear she was not trusted to care for Mr Smithson and that she would pack her belongings and leave Hacket House and Bramley on the next train. Only then did Clarissa relent. Her hands balled into fists, her pale skin scarlet, she had declared that Jane could keep her inferior room if she so wished before storming out, her silken black robe flapping behind her as she slammed the door.

Things had been strained between the two women ever since, and Jane remained deeply suspicious regarding what the hell was going on and what Clarissa did not want her to see. But she had been paid the same wage for less work, so Jane planned to bide her time and find out what Clarissa and the household were up to. She had been unable to find

Dolly again, she had scoured the house for the strange woman, hoping she might be able to shed some light on the situation. But she'd found no sign of her in any of the rooms and Jane was beginning to wonder if she had imagined her after all. The feeling intensified as she found herself standing far too close to the clock, her clock, murmuring her troubles to it as she ran her fingers over its wooden frame. She was going to pieces after too much grief and too little sleep. But logic and reason felt dead to her, as it had since the catastrophic death of Rowena. Here in the red walls of Hacket House, listening to the constant murmurs of the clocks and Mr Smithson's screams, reason not only felt dead, but extinct. It had no place in her mystery. It was just a shame that there were no cute animal companions around, or hot aloof detectives to get infuriated with her. Then she'd be able to tell herself it was just like the books she devoured one after the other and she'd know that it would all turn out alright in the end. She had lost her nerve with the Harry Potter's after the incident in the bakery and returned them to the library. She had listened to them in the nights she'd fed Rowena, repeated the stories to her as the baby snuggled up in her arms. Now they were tainted.

As well as the footsteps in the night, there was the rattle of Mr Smithson that seemed to chill her to the core and tore through her nightmares like some sort of hellish wind. If she didn't know any better, she would have said that the old man was being tortured. Every night she heard him, and in the morning she checked every inch of his flesh, particularly the areas of his body where any injury would be hard to spot. Between his toes and contracted knees and fingers were checked, as was inside his toothless mouth as best she could, and lastly she checked as best she could between his legs and buttocks. Reluctantly she sniffed and for once was reassured by the man's noxious stench, there was no sign of anything, no blood, no marks, no bruises, nothing. No sign that he had been touched or moved at all in the night. Even the clocks were staying put. She could only guess that he was stiff or having cramps or some other pains, or that he was tormented by some sort of night terrors or horrific memories from his past. She had insisted that Clarissa call the doctor who, after a quick peer, Jane was sure he didn't want to get too close to his patient. The doctor declared that Mr Smithson showed no signs of pain and that as Mr Smithson had documented he did not wish to receive medication when he was of sound mind there was nothing to be done. Clarissa agreed and Jane offered to care for him through the night again. Clarissa insisted that whilst she appreciated Jane's dedication, it would not be necessary.

Every night, upon hearing the rattles, she would turn on her lamp and creep from her bed, her heart in her throat. Even after the doctor's and Clarissa's reassurances, she could not help herself. She had to try and go see what the hell was happening, so she'd creep towards the bedroom door and twist the handle, but like a bad dream it would be locked from the outside with a key in the lock and she would be unable to get to him. But did she really want to get to him? Did she want to venture out among the clocks and the strangers? Helplessly, she'd get back into bed and cover her head with the covers, put her headphones on, and listen to White Rabbit on her phone on a loop, blocking out the footsteps and the screams and eventually forcing sleep upon herself. Even as she slept, a heavy weight lying beside her in the bed and the noises of the house would haunt her. Come six am she would wake up and find herself alone in the giant four-poster. Stumbling to the door she would find herself able to open it and she'd rush to Mr Smithson, expecting to find him lying in a pool of blood or with parts of him missing. But he'd be just how he had been when she first came to the house and she'd convince herself that it was all just a nightmare along with the stranger in the bed. After all, no one else in the house seemed bothered by his wails or the stomping of multiple feet. But as each day and night passed, Jane became more and more concerned that what she thought she heard and experienced at night was real. What had started off as fantasies started to form into definite plots, only fear of what she might find held her back.

She looked forward to her weekend off with almost feverish excitement. She was going hiking and camping in the countryside around the village with Molly on Saturday. She couldn't wait to spend time with someone unconnected to the house, away from the clocks and Mr Smithson. Her and Richard had loved to go camping before Rowena was born, and they had planned to take her with them when she was a bit older. Jane hadn't been camping since before Rowena was born, when Richard convinced her that spending the weekend in a tent in Wales whilst six months pregnant would be fun. Looking back, she saw it as typical of Richard's self-centredness. Back then, blinded by love, she'd gritted her teeth, braved the storm, suffered soaked clothes and a leaking tent just so Richard could get his photographs with his overpriced camera. Now she felt a twinge of sadness that she would never take Rowena camping. She knew it was time to build new memories away from other peoples' houses; whilst she saved for her and Rowena's ultimate escape this was a fairly economical way of doing so.

They met in the dining room at 6.30 as usual and Dora had prepared one of her meat pies which she gushed and fussed over as if fussing a beloved pet.

'Now dear, I have a package of sausages, bacon, chops, eggs, and bread wrapped up in the fridge for you. Just pop it in the cool bag in the morning. There are also some potatoes wrapped up next to the cool bag and don't forget you're welcome to take any leftover pie with you.' Jane could almost feel Atticus and Clarissa roll their eyes as Jane was forcibly reminded of Mrs Lovett and wondered if the night time traffic was connected to some underground meat market Dolly and Dora might be running together.

'Erm thanks Dora, I'm not sure what Molly's bringing but I'll take what I can.' Jane smiled at the manically grinning woman who filled her plate with a giant piece of pie.

'Jesus Dora, she's only going into the hills for the night, not trekking over the Himalayas,' observed Atticus, earning himself a significantly smaller piece of pie.

When Dora bustled back to the kitchen for a pot of veg, Jane and Atticus smoothly swapped portions.

'Have you packed the maps of the surrounding area?' Clarissa asked, pouring herself a large glass of wine.

'Yes, I'm all ready to go.'

'Insect repellent and sun cream?'

'Yes, I'm all packed.'

'I have a shot gun you can take in case all that meat attracts a pack of foxes or some passing werewolf? Better be safe than sorry, aye ladies?'

Clarissa glared at Atticus as Dora came in with a steaming pot of veg and Jane laughed.

Dinner passed with a lot of advice from Clarissa and Dora and a number of sarcastic comments from Atticus that made Jane smile. It was actually as if the people around the table cared about her wellbeing, which was particularly nice as Clarissa had been cooler towards Jane since she refused to move rooms. As dinner went on, aided by a small glass of wine Clarissa poured her, Jane found it harder and harder to imagine the people around her would harm anybody, let alone Mr Smithson. Feeling drained and more tired than she had ever felt before, Jane retired to her room. She had been planning to double check her backpack except she felt so drained that she just collapsed on her bed, fully clothed, and slept. It was a dreamless sleep with nothing beside her, undisturbed by screams, clocks, or stomping feet.

The alarm woke her up at six am, it was the alarm on her clock rather than her phone alarm. Every tone on the phone's playlist sounded alien and out of place in the house. For once Jane felt as if she'd had a restful night. *Mr Smithson must have had a restful night too,* she thought as she finally emerged from her bed twenty minutes later.

Her mood improved further as she opened the curtains to discover a bright sunny day without a cloud in the sky. Quickly she dressed in the multi pocket trousers, hiking boots and sweater she had purchased from the outdoors shop in the village and fastened her black hair out of the way in a practical ponytail. She never really got sun burnt, thanks to her father's Jamaican heritage. His parents had immigrated from Jamaica and built new lives for themselves in England, carving a space for themselves and their children amongst the sometimes hostile and mainly pale natives. They lived to see their son marry one, but not long enough to meet Jane, it had always been clear to Jane that they lived on through her dad's memory of them and now they all continued through Jane herself. She had inherited the dark hair and eyes as well as a greater resistance to the sun which her mother had not shared. Out of habit she still applied sun cream to her face and ears though. Her mum had always insisted, just as she had with little Rowena, hell why take the risk? She remembered her mother's peeling red skin and the pain and discomfort she had felt as her burnt skin continued to burn for days on end. Her arms giving off a heat that shocked both her and her father after they'd all spent a hot summer's day together in Wales. Rowena's skin was paler than hers and neither she nor the doting grandma would have ever forgiven her if the same had happened to Rowena's beautiful soft skin.

Regarding her own skin, she knew it may well be a pointless gesture, but it made her feel somehow closer to her mum, who lasted just long enough to get her through the inquest and the trial. Its oily texture and smell brought back memories of Rowena's only summer and pretty little cotton dresses. With a last look at her room, she grabbed her backpack and carried it down to the kitchen, the clocks greeting her as she passed. She ate a hurried breakfast at the kitchen counter as Dora fussed, a strange glint in her eyes that Jane couldn't explain, then accepted the full and heavy cool bag and hugged the older woman goodbye.

Out in the garden, Jane felt the weight of the house and Mr Smithson lift from her. She practically skipped through the high grass and past the red twisted trees. She stopped at the little graveyard that she hadn't even realised she was going towards. The gate she meant to leave the grounds by was a slight detour away so she guessed she must have taken a wrong turn. In the graveyard, crouched by the most recent grave, (she could tell it was by the relative freshness of the stone), was a figure with a dark hood over their head. To Jane's alarm they appeared to be moving something around in the dirt, a bunch of flowers, dead and yellowing, lay discarded beside the grave. Jane could not help but stand there in the long grass, watching the strange figure and wondering who the hell would be in this hidden graveyard at seven am on a Saturday morning. Remembering the gate, Jane found herself creeping forwards, using the trees and thorny bushes for cover. She felt a bit ridiculous, like a tortoise in a cartoon creeping on two legs, but she was too curious, and she dared not leave her bag in case she had to leg it into the undergrowth. She crept around until she could see the gate to the graveyard, which stood ajar, a large metal key on a chain very much like her own dangled from the lock.

Jane's phone vibrated loudly and she turned and took off through the undergrowth without looking back. She reached the gate she had intended to use and unlocked it quickly with her own keys. She'd been through it so many times by now that she knew exactly which worn key fitted the lock. Locking the gate again, Jane began running down the road. She had an uncomfortable feeling that what she had seen was not meant to be witnessed by her or anyone else. A feeling that she had intruded on a private ceremony of some sort. It didn't stop her from wondering about what she had just witnessed and how it was connected to the house.

As arranged, Molly was waiting at the bottom of the road, tapping madly at her phone and wearing her own backpack which looked significantly lighter than Jane's. Molly's head jerked up at the pounding of Jane's boots, the phone disappearing into the waterproof coat.

'Woah, there was no need to run so hard. I wouldn't have minded waiting another five minutes,' smiled Molly as Jane skidded to a halt just past her, breathing hard and dropping to her bum at the edge of the road.

'Sorry...I'm late, I...overslept,' Jane panted.

'Hey there's no hurry. Is this the food Mrs Doyle expects us to eat?' Molly eyed the large cool bag slung across Jane's shoulder.

'Yeah, I think she thinks we might get lost and not be able to find our way home again for a week.'

Molly sighed.

'Ah well, put half in here and we'll carry it together. Molly took off her pack and fished out a small cool bag.

'You sure you don't mind?'

'Not as long as I get to eat my half,' smiled Molly.

Once the food had been divided and Jane had caught her breath, they set off on the route they had already agreed upon, cutting through the still sleeping village, the odd villager they passed waving at her with such enthusiasm that she might be the queen. As they passed the park and Molly continued to talk, Jane couldn't help looking at the deserted swings and climbing frames. With a start, she realised that the normally deserted park was not deserted. A small girl, far too small to be out and alone in such a sinister park, sat perched at the top of the slide, watching them pass the metal fence as Jane's voice caught in her throat and all she could do was watch the small dark-haired girl wave them on.

'Evelyn!' a woman shouted nearby, and the little girl turned and ran off leaving Jane to stare at the cold empty space the girl had once occupied. They carried on through the barely alive streets before going off and up through the woods at the opposite side of Bramley to the house.

The difference was obvious to Jane and breath-taking. It was as if she'd fallen down the rabbit hole into another world, it was that dramatic. Whilst the trees in the house's grounds were rust red, gnarled and twisted as if by a great force, which Jane assumed must be wind, the trees here grew straight up and tall with normal looking greenish leaves and brown bark, the kind of trees that can be found in any forest or street. As they started to climb the gentle slope, Jane who had kept the real reason for her running to herself, commented on the difference between the trees and how much more vibrant the green of the leaves, how richly varied the colours of the bark, even how vital the soil appeared in this wood. It was like she'd just stepped out of a creepy black and red photo into the light.

'Yeah, well some people reckon the house is so haunted that even the plants that grow near it are affected,' Molly said with a slight shudder.

'Is that even possible?' frowned Jane.

Molly shrugged.

'I don't know, Mam reckons it is.'

'There has to be a logical explanation of some sort. The trees at the house must be a special variety and get more wind or less sun or something like that?'

'Maybe,' Molly sounded unconvinced. 'Is it true that Atticus Whiteley actually smiles at you?'

Jane blushed under her friend's knowing smirk.

'You know Mrs Rowling was in the shop getting her perm, she and Mrs Doyle go right back. They were at school together, and Mrs Rowling married Mrs Doyle's brother's best friend. She's been telling us all about how nice Mr Whiteley is to you, how helpful, how he's always smiling now when no one's seen him smile since Mrs Whiteley's death.' Molly's voice practically sang she was so pleased with her information. 'He must really like you and it's easy to see why.'

Jane felt her cheeks scorch up in embarrassment.

'Look, there is nothing going on between Atticus and me, I mean he must be what, fifteen or twenty years older than me. And well, there just isn't!'

'Yeah but he's aged well hasn't he? Still very fit. I bet he might even have a six pack under that shirt!' Molly still smirked, dodging away from Jane as the smaller woman went to push her. 'Hey, he could be your sugar daddy, I bet he has a few quid tucked away.'

'It's not like that, Atticus is kind to me and relatively, well, normal. I can have a normal conversation with him. Dora is sweet but slightly psycho, Clarissa is like some mysterious femme fatale who found herself single in some creepy old house, wondering what the hell happened.'

Molly laughed at Jane's analysis as they followed the now steeper mud path.

'You like him too, don't you?' Molly still smiled but it was a more friendly open smile, less like the smile of a clown who'd taken a hit of laughing gas.

'Well, he is quite handsome in a ruggish, manly sort of way. His voice is quite, well, sexy I suppose. And we get on ok, but nothing will ever happen you know,' Jane said, thinking of her favourite clock and wondering if she was suffering from some sort of fetish. They stopped to rest on a large fallen tree just before the slope took a steeper incline and they'd practically have to climb until they reached the next path. Jane felt freer and more open than she had in years in the fresh morning air as she unearthed a metal water bottle from her pack.

'Why not? You like him, he's crackers for you. You could live in his cottage with him.' Molly still grinned, taking a bite out of a breakfast bar.

'I've never really had much luck with men, and he's not had much luck with women has he? Besides, in a year or two, I'll be somewhere far, far away from here, somewhere hot with beaches, free and single, having holiday flings with hot blond surfer dudes who I'll forget the second they step back on their airplane.'

'Ooh, sound's good. I might come with you.' Molly smiled dreamily, clearly picturing brilliant sunlight and hot young, tanned flesh.

'Hey, you'll have to find your own hot surfer dudes,' Jane grinned at her friend. Both women howled with laughter before Molly insisted on a couple of selfies with Jane before they heaved their packs onto their backs and starting up the steep incline, using the rocky ground as handy foot holds.

Once at the top of the steep slope, the women started up a smaller dirt trail on a gentler slope, going around the hillside instead of straight up. The path took them past lush green fields with grazing sheep and their lambs, and Jane felt a pang of pain seeing the animals with their young. She found herself desperately hoping the animals would never be parted. Molly chattered on, needing only minimal support from Jane, which was one of the reasons she liked her so much. They ate cold leftovers for lunch by a pretty natural waterfall that carved a path through the rock and grass of the hills. Once lunch was over, Molly's phone was out, taking photos of the waterfall, Jane, and the spectacular view. Jane was relieved to find her a quick snapper and not a perfectionist amateur obsessed with the perfect picture. Molly was done in two minutes and going behind a bush. Soon after setting off, they found themselves away from the fields and in woodland again. Jane was somewhat relieved, and they continued their ascent until they reached the summit at about four, when Jane found herself looking straight down at the surrounding countryside and fellow mountains. The view took Jane's breath away, and she could see for miles around. From up here the village looked like a toy town with another toy town behind it that Jane had never been to, but which Atticus had promised to drive her to one day. Eventually Jane found herself looking down at Hacket House; it looked like a haunted dolls house in its black and red grounds. But from her perch on the top of the mountain, a sudden unsettling feeling began to irritate her. From her position, the difference between the house and surrounding land was clearer than it had ever been before. The land belonging to the house was red, blood red in places, the dark leaves almost black in colour, the trees themselves another shade of rich darkness, a patch of decay in the local green area. Looking at it, Jane felt nauseous. This was no freak of nature that some smarter person would logically explain away in a heartbeat. There was something very wrong with Hacket House and its garden and she didn't know what to do.

When Molly returned from behind her rock, the phone disappearing back into its pocket, Jane did her best to pretend that nothing was wrong. Molly, with all the intuition of a brick, as Atticus had described her, didn't seem to notice as she chatted about a man she'd met at the pub the other night as they started their slow part-descent down the other side of the mountain. By five they had found the patch of land Molly had told her about, where they planned to set up their tent.

Having both camped plenty of times before, they made short work of erecting Molly's four man tent ('In case we meet any hot hikers,' Molly had said, but in truth they'd seen no one all day). Next they made a fire and Jane began the cooking. Jane ate the food in a contented silence whilst Molly tapped at her phone whilst simultaneously firing questions then answered them for her. Jane just nodded in agreement. They carried on talking as the darkness of the night settled around them and the birds retired. Jane wondered if there were bats swooping silently through the trees above them as Molly moaned about the mothers group. Apparently their buggies did not just take over the cafe, but also swamped the little shops and Molly's hairdressers in particular, as they 'Stand around talking with their precious brats, as if they're better than everyone else just because they've shat out something living!'.

Jane heard the frustration in Molly's voice, but it was far too dark to see her animated face. Anger welled up inside her, and in that moment she hated the crazy bitch almost as much as she hated Richard. She wondered if they would come across any more steep cliffs tomorrow or what kind of accidents happen by torchlight in the dark.

As an owl hooted overhead Jane excused herself. Using the light of her torch she went behind a tree, when she returned the fire was out and Molly's boots were placed side by side in the opening of the tent. Jane took her own boots off and clambered inside, drifting off to sleep. She woke with a start in total darkness. For a few moments she didn't know where she was or who the hell was snoring a breath away from her? The cold ground and the thin mat she lay on brought her back to her present situation. Lying in a tent in a dark forest near her friend whom she should really drop, possibly off a cliff, Jane fumbled for her torch in the darkness. The little light flared to life against the canvas wall of the tent and all of Jane's anger and hurt was forgotten in an instant. Something large crouched just beyond the flimsy canvas. How she wished for a solid wall as a hideous shape, far too long to be the head of a man and far too reptilian to belong to a dog, emerged from the main bulk of the animal. As it stretched out it became clear that it crouched or stood on all fours. She heard it pant and sniff, something rattling in its lungs as it inhaled so deeply it felt as though it might be attempting to suck the tent, and them trapped inside it, up into its nose.

Jane wondered what kind of mutated wolves had been let loose in this part of the country as she fumbled to switch off the torch. Fear biting at her, she remained as still as her trembling flesh would allow and stared at the canvas where the creature had been, listening closely, expecting the canvas to rip open at any moment. She wished that she'd taken Atticus's shot gun; even if neither of them could shoot, the noise would have probably scared off whatever was out there. Then again, as its shadow suddenly reared up, mouth open, towering over the tent, Jane wondered if anything scared something with that many large teeth and a set of jaws that didn't just open but appeared to dislocate. 'Off with her head,' Grace Slick's haunting voice piped up from somewhere inside and Jane's hand clamped over her mouth to stop herself from screaming. Without the gun, instinct and fear told her their only prayer was to remain still and silent and hope the predator with the long, curved teeth moved on. The creature dropped down onto its four legs, a howl that almost caused Jane to wet herself tore through the night, and Jane screamed into her hands. Then the shadow was gone, and all Jane heard was her own sobbing breaths and Molly's snoring. All there was to do now was tremble in the dark and try to slow her racing heart so that she might hear the beast over her own pounding pulse. She crouched there listening for what felt like forever. But no matter how hard Jane listened, all she heard was Molly. She thought she heard something else, the whisper of something breathing, thought she caught a whiff of something that reminded her of the house. Eventually, slowly and carefully, she laid back down, cursing every little rustle the fabric of her warm sleeping bag made. She felt movement outside the tent and bit back a scream, burrowing deep into the sleeping bag. There was a slight rustle as the creature brushed against the canvas. Jane closed her eyes tight and thought of Rowena and her own mother, certain that death was quickly approaching.

Jane awoke with a start to find that the sun had turned the tent into an oven and was slowly roasting her. Somehow, they'd made it through the night. Jane listened, but all she heard was Molly's voice talking to someone outside the tent. Jane strained to listen, but it sounded like Molly was actually whispering and all she could make out was a low series of mumbles and hisses. Shaking her head, Jane climbed out of her sleeping bag and sat at the edge of the sleeping quarters, lacing up her boots, of course it was gone. The beast had just been a bad dream, like the beast under her bed when she was small or the old man she still sometimes felt on her bed beside her. Nightmares always died in the daylight, whatever that thing was would not be out sunning itself in the morning sun. Of course it hadn't been real, how could anything cast a shadow in a pitch black tent with no light, it just wasn't logical, was it. Despite her logic, her body, tired and tender told her otherwise. Something terrible had happened. Jane shook her head as she tied her boots, her body was clearly lying to her. Jane opened the outer tent flap and crawled out. Molly was sat beside a little fire, cross-legged, phone in hand. Jane noticed that she only wore one boot. Molly offered a too wide grin and the phone disappeared.

'Hey how's sleeping beauty this morning? Did you sleep well? I slept like a brick as usual.' Molly's voice sounded far too cheerful as she flipped the burnt bacon. Jane admired the bright morning and the gorgeous hillside.

'I woke up in the night and it took me a while to get back to sleep. Where's your other boot?'

Jane asked, joining Molly by the fire.

'It's in that tree over there drying, would you believe it. Some wild animal took a giant shit in it!'

Molly said, stretching her mouth again as if there was nothing wrong. Jane's optimism vanished and was replaced by a horrible sinking sensation. For a moment she dared not speak and shuddered despite the warmth of the day, she didn't know whether to laugh or cry that the big animal was not only real but had been right beside their flimsy tent. It had to be some sort of coincidence, didn't it? Jane barely heard a word Molly forced out as they ate breakfast, packed up their tent, and began the descent through the woods. The beast was real, it had not disappeared when the sun rose, it was out there somewhere.

Chapter 10

The descent home was easier than the climb up. They took a number of detours down pretty paths and little country roads that no one seemed to have driven down in decades. At least Jane hoped no one had, as Molly jumped over giant pothole after giant pothole. Jane managed to scatter the remains of the food Dora had given them, as her way of thanking the strange wildlife for not eating them. The beast played on her mind as she looked on at the sheep with their lambs huddled close. She looked carefully in every field but saw no evidence of lone sheep pining for their lambs nor any signs of bloody mayhem. Meanwhile Molly remained glued to her phone, insisting on taking selfies Jane refused to be any part of and doing whatever else she did on the device. Jane wondered how she could talk, jump over and dodge potholes only a tractor could actually drive over, whilst playing with the device and not falling over as they headed downhill, past stone tumbling-down barns and moss-covered walls. It must be a superpower or something.

They sat on a bench looking down towards more stone villages, their needle-like spires pricking at the blue sky, and ate lunch.

'Why doesn't Bramley have a church? All the others seem to,' Jane asked Molly as the realisation hit her and a cold that had nothing to do with the weather caused her to pull the zip of her coat higher. She'd never had much interest in religion or Gods. But why would Bramley be the exception to the rule, all the other villages had churches.

'Oh, it did have a church, in about the 16th century. It was right where the playground is now.'

'What happened to it?'

'The villagers burnt it to the ground one night.'

'What? Why?'

'Oh, they'd recently had a new priest. Well, after his arrival strange things started to happen. The village found out that he had corrupted their church.'

'What do you mean corrupted it?' Jane felt a tingling sensation as she forced herself to take a bite out of the sausage roll Dora had packed.

'You know, written blasphemy on the walls in sheep's blood and shit. Declaring his loyalty to Satan. Turning all the crosses upside down, the usual weird stuff. My sister told me he made the Christ on the Cross a huge dildo from pig's skin. Asked his parishioners to blow Christ when they took communion. That he used to have a black goat called Joseph who used to bone him on the alter before Sunday service.' Molly's eyes gleamed as she described the priest's activities, clearly delighted to be sharing such an unsavoury story. Jane shook her head.

'That can't be true, that has to be a story surely?' Molly shrugged her shoulders.

'My sister said it was true, she did a big project on the history of Bramley Village and found loads of buried shit like that. She won't talk about it again, burnt all her research and buggered off to Australia. But she told me, after a few drinks before she went.'

'But every school kid knows that the church burnt down in the 16th century. The school doesn't teach that the village started the fire with the goat and the priest locked inside.'

'Was it completely destroyed?' Jane asked, giving up on lunch just as Molly had given up on her phone.

'Pretty much, a few stones remained. Some of the villagers stole them and used them in their houses or walls. You can still see them to this day,' Molly said, checking the time on her phone.

'There's a pub just down the hill. Do you want to go for a drink?'

Jane nodded; she could use a drink after that.

The pub was a tiny little lopsided stone house that looked like it was sliding down the hill. They went inside and Molly ordered a couple of pints of locally produced cider. The fizzy liquid tingled in Jane's mouth as she leaned back against the wooden pew. Gradually the women began to relax, Molly's phone lay forgotten on the table as she spoke about her terrible luck with online dating and how all the men she met locally turned out to be hopeless deadbeats. They ordered more cider and Molly told Jane about discovering her ex had been chasing other women on his online game. Jane comforted her and ordered more cider, and to her surprise found herself telling Molly about Richard, how they had been a couple for four years and that Richard had done the worst thing in the world to her and broken her heart, that she would never ever forgive him!

'Oh, come on! It can't be as bad as sending dick picks,' Molly slurred, her eyes gleaming at what promised to be the juiciest piece of gossip she would hear all year. Jane looked into Molly's eyes as tears ran down her face and realised that Molly couldn't wait to share what Richard did with everyone who came into the hairdressers. Hate and hurt sobered her up and Jane ordered more drinks. She managed to distract Molly with a few questions and Molly was soon happily cursing the whole male sex and swearing eternal celibacy.

The rest of the journey was relatively uneventful. Molly sent some man she was meant to be meeting an abusive message and together, arm in arm, they stumbled down the hill. Sticking to the little roads that only ever saw the occasional tractor or escaped sheep, Jane saw Molly to her parents' house. They said goodbye, clinging to each other like soul mates before Molly flopped onto the sofa and started snoring. She'd had a few more drinks than Jane and it showed. Jane was still drunk and very tired when she made it back to the house at 6.15. The red wood structure loomed up on its wild, dark red land which was the colour of dried blood and scabs. Exposed bone held the house steady for her. The clock chimed to welcome her home and despite everything, she found herself glad of the safety, the solid walls and relative quiet it provided. She stepped through the front door and walked slowly and carefully up the winding staircase, pulling herself along by the banister. She met no one on her journey.

In the safety and cool of her bedroom, Jane collapsed fully clothed onto her bed and fell into a deep black sleep. When she awoke, she was dismayed to discover that it was already eight pm and she was late for dinner. That didn't matter, she still had some food from earlier and didn't feel much like the company of Dora or Clarissa. Looking out of her window into the garden, Jane found that it was still light outside. An evening stroll around the garden was just what she needed. Without changing, Jane left the house through the back door, skirting around the sullen decayed statues and dry fountain. She walked into the deep undergrowth of the silent and still garden, admiring the twisted trees and the deeply scarred bark that clung to them like armour. As she rounded a corner, she was just in time to see a tall thin figure dart behind a solitary rain-scarred statue.

Chapter 11

For a number of seconds that felt like hours, Jane stood still. Her heart hammered against her rib cage as an old fear gripped her. Who the hell was that? She debated what she should do, then her feet made the decision for her and she took off running, behind the stone monument and into the thorny and dense undergrowth behind it. The thorns and branches snagged her clothes as she struggled through, managing barely more than a fast walking pace. They snagged and scratched any uncovered flesh they found but Jane barely felt them as she struggled onwards. They couldn't have got far in this. Something too close for comfort, this side of the veil was too close for comfort, howled in the fading light as Jane forced her way out of the thorn patch and fell to her knees in a grass clearing. She let out a strangled cry, suddenly sure that whatever had hung around their tent and pooed in Molly's shoe had followed her home. The creature howled again and Jane was on her feet. She ran through the dark grass that seemed far wetter than the grass in the rest of the garden, the trees when she reached them were not just scarred but had great gouges and craters ripped from their trunks. Some even seemed to have been arranged in such a way that gave the impression of faces, dark red blood…no, sap, it had to be sap which stained the wood.

Jane no longer cared who she had seen as she ran in this nightmare. She was sure that those twisted red faces watched her and followed her. She had to get back to the house and the path between the trees was the easiest. If only she knew which direction the house was in. But God, it had been made out of these monstrous trees! The realisation hit her as she came to the end of the row of trees and skidded to a halt. Blocking her way was a giant slab of blackened ancient wood. Nothing grew on it or anywhere around it for about six feet, the slab stood crooked in tar-like mud in every direction. The slab itself appeared perfect; there was no sign of rot nor woodworm nor even a woodpecker. Jane bet that if she were to dig through the mud she would find no insects, nor worms of any kind. Jane shuddered. What terrible place was this that not even these trees, nor any life whatsoever, would touch it? She felt sure the wood must have been erected a long time ago, long enough for gravity to start pulling it towards the mud. The name carved on the front was clear enough to read from Jane's position six feet away.

'An Erazmus Nark.' The inscription underneath read, 'May he remain forever in this dirt.'

The cold words made Jane shudder again. It wasn't just the loveless, soulless words for someone unworthy of peace who may or may not have the decency to stay in his grave. Jane was sure the weather was colder here, and she zipped up her coat.

'They must have buried him here because it's not consecrated ground,' Jane thought as she picked her way around the grave, clinging to the monstrous trees to prevent herself slipping in the mud and sliding any closer to the hideous monument, whilst also keeping it in sight. Jane was suddenly deeply afraid of what could happen if she turned her back on it or slipped and fell in the swamp of mud. Would she be able to get out of it again? Or would it suck her under into some hidden rabbit hole to join the loathsome Erazmus Nark? Her gut told her that the mud would swallow her whole, make her disappear and any trace of Rowena with her. It was the thought of Rowena, lost forever in the terrible mud, that clamped Jane's body and hands to the twisted red trees. The wood was warm and surprisingly soothing against her hands that now throbbed with pain. Jane looked at them and was shocked to discover long scratches scarred her flesh and left their own stains against the now comforting and somehow empathising trees.

By the time she was away from the slab and back among the protection of the trees, the light was fading fast. The sight of the house brought tears to Jane's eyes as the last of the light clung on and another howl tore open the sky.

What the hell kind of beasts live around here? Jane thought as her key scraped against the metal lock of the dark door that seemed to loom over her. It could be her imagination, but in the gloom Jane fancied that the rich varnish had a blood red tint. As the last of the light faded and a far closer howl tore at Jane, her key suddenly turned and she fell through the large front door, sprawling onto the thick rug. Gasping, Jane wondered if the rug was there just for this purpose.

'Good evening Jane, I was expecting you home earlier,' a familiar voice said as a harsh light illuminated the gloomy hall. It should not be possible for a person on all fours to jump, but Jane managed it. Gasping, she allowed Clarissa to help her to her feet, and as her eyes adjusted to the light of the hall it became a comforting glow. The familiar clocks were oddly guardian-like as they loomed around them.

'I was, then I went for a walk. Did you hear that howling?' Jane managed to gasp. Clarissa looked as gaunt and dignified as ever, standing encased in a figure-hugging black dress, her long hair neatly scraped away from her face. 'I wouldn't go out if I were you, something is out there.'

'Oh, that is just Mr Jonas's new guard dog. He got a beast of an animal to protect his farm from foxes. Frightful man, always overreacting, we will have the beast removed if it proves to be too much of a nuisance,' Clarissa stated, looking Jane up and down with a critical hooded eye.

'You must be exhausted! Why don't you go up and have a bath and an early night? I can have Dora send you up some super and a glass of wine if you require.'

'I will, thanks. How has Mr Smithson been?'

'The same as always, though I must admit the temporary carer does not have your diligence. We will not be hiring her again.'

'Oh, I can start tonight if you want-'

'Nonsense, you enjoy the rest of your time off.' Clarissa forced a smile and Jane thought how tired and tense the other woman looked before she turned away from her and headed towards one of the drawing rooms.

'Wait Clarissa,' a sudden urge propelled Jane to speak. Clarissa turned to face her, an eyebrow raised.

'Who looks after the garden?'

'Why, no one. I am afraid we have experienced a great many difficulties keeping gardening staff and Atticus is far too busy caring for the generators and the house.'

'Well, would it be alright if I had a go at looking after it? Well, at least bits of it?'

'Why of course, make yourself at home.' Clarissa smiled again, this time there was humour in it and Jane was certain that she was enjoying a private joke at her expense. With that, Clarissa swept where she had been heading, closing the door behind her with a snap. Jane stood for a moment, working up the energy for the climb to her bedroom. She thought she heard Clarissa's muffled voice through the door, but too tired to care, Jane turned and trudged upstairs.

Resisting the urge to collapse back onto the bed, she forced herself to run a bath with plenty of bubble bath. As she lowered herself into the hot water, her muscles soothed and relaxed. She had always enjoyed long hot baths, they had become a special treat after Rowena was born. Since her death, she had denied herself them, yet another small way of punishing herself. Lying in the water, she thought of Rowena, memories that had remained buried under her pain and grief; Rowena's laughter and the goofy smile that had lit up her little face and Jane's heart, the small figure chasing her mum's elderly cat around the garden. The poor thing was old and lazy, its world brought into chaos by the small chubby figure in dungarees. Rowena always looked so adorable in them that Jane could never resist buying her a new pair. Jane had always suspected the old boy was really as fond of Rowena as the baby was of him. Her first and only word had been cat. Richard had never liked that, she could still remember that tight smile he pulled, that he thought hid his displeasure and fooled everyone. And it had fooled her, in the beginning. Only her mum had seen through it, of course. He'd always hated cats. Darker memories chased away the screaming, laughing toddler. Suddenly it was all cold grey hospitals and police stations with dark windowless interview rooms where cold grey men interrogated her, as if the beautiful child's death was not already the end of the world as she knew it. They told her, with relish, that it was caused by someone. That someone had shaken her little body with such violence that she might have been in a car crash. And that if *she* hadn't shaken the baby till her neck snapped, then who could it have been? The bastard had at least had the decency to look embarrassed as she vomited down her jumper and roared in grief and heartbreak.

No longer relaxed, but feeling the righteous anger she'd worked so hard to bury, she got out of the bath, practically rubbing the skin off her flesh with the towel and slung on her pyjamas. She strode into the bedroom, all tiredness forgotten, and slammed the door as hard as she could. Standing before her Gryffindor four-poster bed, she let out a scream of rage, sweeping the books off her shelves and hurling them across the room. Then when the stupid fucks had worked out it was handsome Richard with his white teeth and stupid Captain America good looks they'd got sloppy and lost vital fucking evidence that allowed the baby murdering son of a bitch to walk out of court a free man and forced her into fucking hiding. In a frenzy she screamed, cried, flung everything she owned around her room and tore the pages from her books.

'If I'd married a black man who murdered our baby would they have lost the evidence?' Jane wondered for the millionth time as she screamed herself hoarse and yanked at her hair as if attempting to scalp herself, as if the physical pain could sooth her psychological torture.

At last she felt calmer, calm enough to hear that there had been another scream, a scream that had not been her own. She threw on her dressing gown, swung the door open, cracking the metal handle against the wood panel, and strode down the corridor. The mood she was in she was ready to take on anyone, the watching clocks knew it too, she could tell as they leaned away from her ticking quietly. She was sure they were ticking quieter than normal, as if they hoped to avoid her wrath. How dare they accuse her of killing her beautiful daughter with the goofy grin and button nose? She'd have died for her, she'd have died if it would give Rowena the chance to live and be loved again. Hell, no price would be too much to pay to get Rowena back. She was striding towards Mr Smithson's door, there was no more screaming but strange voices came from behind it. Ready for anything, Jane threw the door open and stepped inside. She thought she had been ready for anything, but she was wrong. Twenty or so people knelt around the nursing bed that housed the remains of Mr Smithson. He blinked back at her, his toothless mouth hanging open as it usually did. Every one of them wore a heavy black cloak that covered their head, face, and body. The only one not wearing a black cloak was stood at the head of the nursing bed, the woman with the straw-coloured mass of hair and burning eyes set in dark sockets whom Clarissa had denied existed. She was the only one who hadn't moved. Despite their hoods, Jane could tell that the people on their knees had all turned to stare at her, the intruder, as had the clocks around the cult.

Chapter 12

Jane just stood there and stared at the figures. They seemed to stare back as she felt their eyes bore into her and her cheeks flush. To Jane it was like being in a room surrounded by Deatheaters, like she'd fallen headfirst into the Harry Potter universe and found herself surrounded by torturers and killers. Right now, in what should be the real world, Jane didn't know if the Deatheaters planned to kill or curse her or expected her to leave and pretend she'd never seen them. She wasn't going anywhere, they were in her world not theirs. The house was her home and Mr Smithson was her service user/patient/client or whatever the latest buzz word someone somewhere had decided would give dignity to someone lying in a bed shitting themselves uncontrollably. Whatever she should call him, she cared about Mr Smithson, he relied on her and she wouldn't leave him now. So, there she stood, as straight and assertively as she could, wondering what the next move would be. If she screamed for help they could be on her in seconds. Besides, she did not know for sure who was and who wasn't under the hoods. It could be that she alone was the only resident of Hacket House, along with Mr Smithson, not hidden by a fantasy cloak.

It was one of the figures on the right who moved first, standing up and sweeping past her without a word. The other cloaked figures followed, none spoke to her nor looked directly at her. Only the woman with the straw-coloured hair remained, unmoving, staring down at the old man. Jane stepped forwards, a horrid sense of dread lingering in the air. It seemed to be coming from the strange woman and the bed where Mr Smithson lay. As the rattle began again Jane noticed the stench for the first time and almost gagged.

'I have to change him now.' The words seemed to have come from her mouth, but she'd had no intention to speak.

The woman didn't respond and for a moment Jane wondered if she had imagined the sound of her own voice. Then, with a crack and a terrible grinding noise, the woman snapped her neck to the side and glared at Jane. It was such a malevolent look that Jane's resolve faltered and she stopped half way across the room. The woman bared her teeth in a snarl and Jane saw they were blackened and decayed. From the woman's mouth came the sound of grinding and she stared fixated at the rotating jaw and creaking teeth. The noise got louder and louder and Jane found herself back at the door with her hands over her ears. When she could bear looking at the woman no longer, her eyes snapped shut and she waited, waited for the rotten mess of teeth to fasten itself to her jugular and pull. Waiting for the woman to strike, Jane thought of Rowena. Eventually, when nothing happened, she lifted her hands from her ears slightly and found the terrible grinding had stopped. The terrible sense of dread remained however and eventually Jane was forced to ignore it and open her eyes a crack. She found herself staring straight into the bottomless burning eyes of the woman. Then the world went completely black and Jane felt herself falling.

Jane found herself lying on the floor of the bedchamber. The back of her head throbbed, as did something she expected was her heart in the top of her throat. She sat up with a start and scanned the room in the dim light as far as she could, listening closely and straining her senses in the semi-gloom. When she thought they were alone, she pulled herself up to her feet and fumbled for the main light switch at the side of the door, the glare of the light illuminating the room and Mr Smithson in the bed just as she remembered him. Even the clocks were now in their normal positions, even though she could have sworn she had neither seen nor heard anybody move them. Calling Mr Smithson's name softly, she crossed the room and further examined him. His covers had been removed and all he wore was his pad and netty knickers. His forehead burned against her trembling hand. Looking into his eyes Jane took a step back and stared. For a number of minutes, Mr Smithson's normally grey eyes appeared so dark they were almost black, they glared at Jane with a level of hatred and malevolence that was far too personal for comfort. It reminded Jane of Richard's court case, as he shrank before her glare. Had her own eyes looked similar?

After a few moments, Mr Smithson's eyes were their normal empty grey. Feeling his skin, she found it to be cold and clammy. After she dried him with a towel, she manoeuvred a loose t-shirt over his contracted arms and sticking out bones. She checked his pad and found that he was both wet and soiled. His waste emitted a stench far greater than normal and reminded Jane of rotten, long-dead animals and brought to mind the grave of Erazmus Nark, although she couldn't explain why. Holding her breath, she cleaned him up and covered him in fresh sheets and blankets before giving him as much of his thickened juice as he would drink. He drank far more than normal before closing his eyes and appearing to drift off. Quietly, Jane switched all the lamps off that had illuminated the figures, as well as the main light, and left the room with the wet wipes and plastic pad tied securely in a plastic bag. Holding it at arms' length, she made her way through the house and deposited the bag in an outside bin; there was no way she was going to leave it to stink out the house. What the hell had the other carer been feeding him? Coming back through the house, Jane came across Clarissa in the main hallway, hanging up her designer coat. Jane watched her place it on a coat hanger before opening the hall cupboard and hanging it inside. Then she pulled out a pair of flat court shoes and closed the door. She sat on a hall chair and kicked off her far too high shoes with the red soles. Jane heard her sigh as she freed her feet from her position in the darkened hallway. Clarissa put on the flat shoes that Jane knew she wore around the house and picked up her high heels. Standing up Clarissa happened to glance in her direction and it caused Jane some pleasure to see her start.

'Oh Jane, I didn't see you there! Did you enjoy your bath?'

'Who were all those people in Mr Smithson's room?'

Clarissa's smile faltered.

'What people? There shouldn't be anyone in Mr Smithson's room? What were you doing there?' Clarissa folded her arms across her chest and Jane's temper flared.

'The twenty or so people in black hoods and robes kneeling around his bed like some sort of evil cult! I was checking on him because he was screaming, and you said my replacement was crap.'

The two women glared at one another. It was Clarissa who looked away first and fiddled with her handbag.

'There is a nunnery, a few miles from here, hidden in the trees. Mr Smithson, when he was well, was very kind to them. He donated frequently to the order and, well, they believe that he might be suffering. They make frequent requests to visit Mr Smithson and pray for his soul. Dora lets them in, I know it's a bit backward, but it can't do any harm can it?'

'Well, he didn't seem to like them. He was screaming fit to wake the dead in that graveyard. When I came over he was uncovered and naked except for his netties and pad and he glared at me as if it was me who was the devil, come to torment him.' Jane saw Clarissa flinch. Too angry to care, she spun around and stormed back up the stairs. Halfway up, Jane stopped and turned back to Clarissa.

'Oh yeah and I think that relative of Dora's needs professional help, not to be locked up here. I'm no mental health carer but there is something badly wrong with that woman.' Jane turned back and continued up.

'And take her to a fucking dentist!' With that Jane reached the landing and stomped off ignoring the protests of the wood beneath her feet.

Jane was almost certain that Clarissa was lying, those people were definitely not nuns or anything remotely holy. If they were, they would have come at her with their fake kindness and asked her to pray with them. She'd met enough men and women of God to last her a lifetime. She'd grown up in a Christian household, her mother had prayed every night before bed and had attended the same church for the last ten years where Richard's own mother and father also went. Oh yes, she remembered the men and women of God, eager to pray for her baby's soul one minute and forgiving her father for his terrible 'accident' the next. Just because he said some stupid little words about how he'd found God again and how sorry he was, as if her beautiful Rowena had been the guilty one! What little faith had survived into adulthood had died right there whilst Richard, who'd always been a committed atheist, conveniently found his 'faith' from the remand prison cell and the blind fools had rallied around him!

It was also clear to Jane that Dora's relative was potentially dangerous as well as being neglected and needing to be housed somewhere more suitable. She'd had little experience with mental health care other than dementia and wasn't that sure about the support available, but she was sure there was something better out there than ambling around an old house and being taken advantage of by whoever the freaks in the robes were. She'd have to have a serious talk with Dora, she'd be just the kind of relative who'd think they could care for their own, come what may. Well she clearly couldn't. She'd ask her about the so called 'nuns' too.

That night painful memories taunted Jane, preventing her from sleeping. She got up and was relieved to find that she could unlock her door and wander the corridors. She passed no one, nor found the woman she was almost sure was Dolly, only the clocks who stood watch over the night and gave Jane a sense of comfort. She visited her favourite clock and marvelled at the thing's physique, whoever had chiselled such rippling muscle tones into a clock's body was clearly an artist. The presence of such wordless beauty seemed to calm her spirits. On her way back to her room she checked on Mr Smithson and found him alone with his clocks and sound asleep, whatever had happened with the hooded figures long forgotten. Jane wished that she could forget as easily as she tucked the blanket around him. It was a chilly night and the wind rattled the windows. Listening carefully, she thought she heard the strange howls, but the wind was so fierce she couldn't be certain. She reached her bedroom door and abruptly changed her mind - she wasn't ready to face it just yet and proceeded down the corridor, sensing the clocks confusion.

The library was even chillier than Mr Smithson's bedroom. Nevertheless, she pulled her dressing gown tightly around her and started her search of the high bookshelves. It was a long search, but she pulled out anything she could find relating to the house, Mr Smithson, and the local area. She found a surprising number of books and went through them painstakingly at the oversized desk clearly built from the same red wood as the clocks and everything else. She found no record of any Erazmus Nark in any of them. Bitterly disappointed, Jane painstakingly returned each book to the correct shelf. It was now five am and, determined to check on Mr Smithson again, Jane left the library, taking care to switch off the light and close the door tightly so that no one but the clocks need know of her nocturnal investigations.

Chapter 13

Over the next few weeks Jane did her best to settle back into the ordinary routine of the house. She had confronted Dora the next day and the woman had burst into tears, apologising to Jane and saying that her 'dear Dolly' would be moving to a small supported living house in a nearby village. She swore on her mother's grave that Dolly wouldn't hurt a fly and that the hooded figures were indeed nuns. It was a convincing performance, Jane had to admit, to the extent she wondered if the hooded figures really had been nuns. Maybe she was just prejudiced by the sheep at her mum's church whose betrayal in their support of Richard had hastened her mother's death? Jane didn't know any more.

Every night at seven she had dinner with Clarissa, Dora and Atticus in the dining room. Dora still fussed, occasionally dropping news about Dolly and how well she was doing in her new home. Dolly had been seen by the dental hospital and was much more settled after having most of her teeth removed. The provider was looking into taking Dolly on holiday with another lady at the property. Jane was happy for Dolly, and despite the lump their last meeting had left on the back of her head she sincerely wished Dolly well. Clarissa maintained a professional politeness that was almost painful. Jane knew it was because of the figures in hoods and Dolly, and she felt a mixture of discomfort, determination, and anger. What relationship the two had made tentative steps to form seemed to have frozen and appeared to be on the brink of shattering completely. It was a shame, but Jane resented being lied to about Dolly and hated that the will of whoever wore the hoods had been placed above the welfare of Mr Smithson.

By contrast, Jane's relationship with Atticus seemed to be growing every day. After dinner, as Dora knitted and Clarissa drank, read or played the piano, she and Atticus would play board or card games, occasionally doing jigsaws as they talked. In the day Jane spent most of her spare time in the gardens. She'd started just out in front of the house on a square of ground to the left of the front door. Wearing Atticus's heavy-duty work gloves, she pulled up the oddly red stinging nettles, ripped out the tangled clumps of weeds and removed the mass of dead thorns. Everything was placed in a wheelbarrow, when it was full either she or Atticus would roll it to a clump of land out of the way and dump it in the compost bin Clarissa had allowed them to order. When he was free, Atticus would come and help Jane and they'd toil together, sweating and filthy until their respective jobs called them away or the light faded.

As the days and weeks went by, they cleared the first patch then moved onto the next, then another until they had cleared the garden immediately in front of the house and the watching clock. Every night Jane dropped exhausted into bed and slept right through, undisturbed by nightmares, screams in the night or nocturnal cults. The sensation of a warm body beside her in the bed bugged her otherwise contented rest occasionally, but that was all; in the morning she remained alone in the bed and she just put it down to ghosts from care jobs been and gone. Indeed, she was starting to feel that everything until the present had just been a bad dream from which she had only just awoken. One day, unable to put off a trip to the village any longer, Jane headed out after her morning toast. She had cleared enough debris to fill four compost bins, and now she needed something to fill the void in the dark red crawling earth. For some reason her companions seemed less than enthusiastic about her plans. Clarissa had looked amused by the mere suggestion, almost choking on her morning milk, and both Dora and Atticus had tried to dissuade her from planting. Just as she was about to bite Dora's head off for suggesting that the garden was too much extra work, Atticus had suggested that they build some decking out of the trees on the estate or a nice sculpture. Jane had to admit that she liked the sound of the sculpture, but she wanted it further in the garden. Caught in secret garden fever, she had set her heart on creating her own healthy, blossoming garden.

It had been so long since Jane had walked the path from the estate to the village that she took a couple of wrong turns. She even found herself back at the grave of Nark in the twisted den of trees. She remembered how frightened she had been the last time she was here, how she had run through the thorns as if something evil chased at her heels. Today, in the glorious sunshine, there was nothing to be afraid of, just the noble trees that she would definitely not be turning into decking. She hadn't thought of Nark since she began work on the garden and felt a pang of guilt that she had done so little to investigate the mysterious grave.

Eventually she located the gate, which seemed a good less stiff than she remembered, and started down the country road into the little town. As she walked past, she felt the stares and well-meaning smiles glare at her. She tried to return their smiles but that just felt even stranger. Head down, Jane scurried through what should have been a pleasant walk in the sweet cool breeze. Suddenly Jane realized her feet had taken her to the deserted playground Molly said was once a church. The street beside the park was dead and she was relieved to not be under anyone's grinning scrutiny. Jane hurriedly scanned the cursed playground, the strange little girl at the front of her mind. The playground was deserted, and with growing unease and a shudder that had nothing to do with the breeze, Jane turned away and hurried up the street away from the park and the war memorial.

Jane wondered about Molly, they'd messaged a couple of times, but Jane never wanted to leave the garden long enough to meet up. As she hurried past a manically grinning Mr Hubbs, who had stepped out of a doorway and into her path so quickly that she almost collided with him, she fired off a message and hurried on down the lane. At the main street, Jane bought lots of packets of seeds from the very bemused man with the red nose in the gardening supply shop then hurried along.

'What you want them for? No rose, especially white, would be seen dead in that garden,' Mr Owens half laughed, half barked at her. He was still laughing as Jane left the shop. She was relieved to find that Molly had messaged her back and they were going to have lunch at the bakery during her lunch hour. Looking at her phone, she found she still had twenty minutes before she was due to meet Molly and hurried into the library.

The librarian, smiling from ear to ear, was happy to direct her to the local history section, where she found a number of interesting looking books. Skimming through their indexes she found nothing on Nark. But skimming through a self-published book on the history of local families, she was forced to stop dead and double check that she had read it correctly. The book contained the family trees of all the local landowning families along with other useful information about how much they owned and how much they earned. The book was a mere two years old and seemed to suggest that Clarissa was Mr Smithson's daughter-in-law, married to his only child, Clive. Jane read on, eager for more details. There was no mention that Clive was dead or that Clarissa and Clive had separated. The book only mentioned that the couple lived happily in London with their two cats. Jane was photocopying the family tree when her phone rang and she was forced to hurry past the Cheshire Cat grin of the librarian, leaving the library and the book behind to meet Molly. Out of breath, her eyes gleaming with long forgotten curiosity, Jane found Molly in the bakery and the two hugged. Jane silently thanked the stars above that Molly seemed normal. Molly couldn't wait to hear what had so excited her friend. Jane could see it in her eager smiling face and was immediately wary, the last thing she needed was for what she knew to get back to Clarissa and for her to lose her job, Atticus and her garden. Jane ordered a home made lemonade and a sandwich, Molly had already ordered a pot of tea, despite the glorious day, and a Cornish pasty.

'I found a grave in the garden up at the house.'

'Wow! Really? Why would there be a grave up there?' Molly asked between bites of pastry.

'I don't know, I thought it might be a family grave. But the head stone doesn't have the family name.'

'Ooh, what does it say?'

'Erazmus Nark- a groundskeeper maybe, or a distant family relative. Have you heard of him?'

'No but it's spooky isn't it?'

'Very.'

'Just think, if you stay at the house long enough, maybe they'll bury you up there too.'

'As long as they don't dig up any of my plants.'

They carried on talking, Jane about her plans for the garden and Molly about the village gossip, the hairdressers, and her latest disastrous online date. Jane almost choked on her lemonade as Molly described her date presenting her with a giant cucumber then taking her to the twenty four-hour supermarket twenty miles away for a Saturday night date. She'd forgotten how good it was to have a friend who made her laugh until she choked. All too soon it was time for Molly to go back to the shop and Jane walked with her.

'Hey, are you on Facebook? Molly asked as they hugged goodbye.

'No.'

'Why don't you join? We can keep in touch easier and there's loads of paranormal groups who may know more about the house and if Nark had anything to do with the weird rumours.'

'I like to keep a low profile. My ex was an arsehole and I don't want to make it too easy for him to find me.'

'He won't, there are all sorts of privacy settings now. You can control exactly who sees what. You shouldn't let him stop you joining.'

'Yeah maybe, I'll think about it.'

'Everyone's on it now. Even my mam!' With a laugh Molly went into the salon and Jane hurried off back towards the house.

Chapter 14

A number of weeks went by. The season began to change and it got colder, windier and wetter. The grass and leaves on the trees grew a deeper, darker shade of red as did the wood of the house. The smell of wet wood seemed to haunt Jane. It wasn't just the normal smell of wet wood, it was something else, something underneath that the smell of wet wood masked. Something Jane couldn't quite put her finger on and which the rest of the house denied smelling. Worse than the smell was the ticking and chiming of the clocks, and Jane was sure that they had all gotten louder and more intrusive. Even her old favourite. No one else at the house would admit that either but Jane was sure Clarissa and Dora were just lying to her face. Only Atticus looked away when he lied to her, blushing the ugly ruddy colour she hated to see. She was deeply disappointed by Atticus's denials and avoidance of the subject. He was no longer welcome to join her at her work in the garden where she now spent almost every waking hour when she did not need to be in the house. He did still work on the garden, she knew that, and sometimes she'd come out and see some little change, such as rubbish having been moved to the compost bin or another small area now devoid of weeds. Jane wasn't sure what to make of it. Every day when she was at the house, she saw Atticus at dinner and they'd smile at one another and make polite, meaningless conversation. She never asked Atticus about his help and he never mentioned it. It just remained an unspoken pact between the two of them. If only he'd admit that something really weird was going on and help her out.

If she wasn't in the garden then she would usually be in the town, either at the bakery or in the pub. She was drinking regularly for the first time since she was a teenager, and every morning she woke with a taste in her mouth almost as foul as the stench of the house. She did her best to ignore the villagers who seemed to be turning stranger with each visit. They had long since stopped grinning at her and speaking to her.

Now they just glowered at her, refusing to speak to her even when she ordered something, slamming down her drink or pasties and sullenly waiting for her to put her money on the counter. The sudden change in behaviour played on her mind when she let it. It reminded her of some of the horror stories her father had shared with her. She would have assumed racism, but it wasn't like she'd changed colour or anything. She wondered if the far right had colonised the village of Bramley, but she saw no posters, no demonstrations, no graffiti. Nothing. The only posters she saw were for local events and missing animals. Some days, as she passed more and more posters, it seemed that every animal in the village had gone missing. Maybe someone was spreading nasty rumours about her, but Molly denied hearing anything and no one else in the village would speak to her. Despite the hostile silence, being in the village was better than being in the house. At least the voices she heard were human, raging about various things, especially in the pub where she drank alone. When she had first gone to the pub it was all stories about farming and livestock. Then about farming accidents and adultery. Now it was all men being trampled by livestock, pets disappearing and teenage orgies in the deserted park and its graveyard. Some nights she took a detour and staggered past the deserted monstrosity and looked through the bars. Some nights she heard laughter and saw the glow of multiple cigarettes, other nights the park glowed empty under the moon and Jane drunkenly wondered who'd painted parts of the slide red.

At the garden she had cleared a large patch of ground in front of the house, however the ground remained dark and barren. She had planted the seeds and little plants she had brought from the town into the sodden earth, but the seeds never sprouted, the little plants, no matter what she did, just seemed to rot in the earth, as did the bulbs.. It had to be the weather, she decided. She had just chosen a bad time of year to plant things, that was all. That had to be it, so she kept clearing the garden, preparing the earth for future planting and keeping the encroaching weeds and red vicious nettles at bay as they started to slowly creep back over the black earth. She only wished that her own plants were as persistent.

As she cared for Mr Smithson, she spoke of her problems with the garden and complained about the village, even as the clocks, louder and more overbearing than ever before, looked on. He didn't respond but she felt that both him and the clocks were listening. One day, as she was trying to convince Mr Smithson to take his drink, (he had become less willing to eat and drink over the weeks), Jane recalled what Clarissa had said about the clocks when she first arrived at the house,. about them being made from wood found on the estate. For some reason, surrounded by its damp smell, this struck her as crucially relevant, like one of the jigsaw pieces of the puzzles she and Atticus came together to assemble. As she thought out loud Mr Smithson took a spoonful of juice finally and finished the drink. After his meal and other needs had been attended to, she examined the wood of the clocks with renewed interest as they seemed to purr along. Jane fancied she saw some of the wilder patterns beneath the varnish and a resemblance between them and her favourite trees. The trees she intended would eventually become statements in her garden.

On wet windy nights when the wind, rain and the smell kept her up, Jane found herself using the house's Wi-Fi, searching the internet for Erazmus Nark. She found nothing, but hinted myths came up on the search engines. Myths of terrible torture, supernatural monstrosities and demonic possession turned up. Jane read every bloody, gruesome, improbable page, but none of them mentioned Erazmus Nark. She would always lie in her bed with the bedside lamp on after her research, watching strange shadows dance across her walls and ceiling. She no longer locked her door, it didn't seem important, as no lock could keep out the shadows or the lingering smells.

Arriving home from the pub one evening, she found the shadows had spread from her room and that now the halls of the house were alive with twisting, wriggling shadows which reminded her of the fat juicy worms in the red soil below them. She stumbled along the corridors pretending not to see, praying it was just that last gin and tonic not agreeing with the cider she'd drank earlier. Even as she curled up under her blankets, praying for the shadows to be gone, she knew that her prayers wouldn't be answered. Waking up the next day with the foul taste of what she'd drank the night before threatening to erupt from her, she found the twisting shadows were still there, their constant movement doing nothing for her nausea. Later in the day, as she began to feel more alive, she found that they were less frenzied and that she could watch them hiding in the long shadows of the clocks. Every so often she'd catch one dart across the wall to the next clock and see it try to hide, tucked in close against its new protector.

One wet and windy night, as the single glazing rattled and Jane, unable to sleep, had exhausted yet another internet search for Nark, the smell became such that she moved on to searching for gasmasks on eBay. She was reading the adverts when she heard a voice cry out in the night. It stopped and Jane held her breath, praying silently that she wouldn't hear it again, and that she could just go back to her internet search without having to investigate. She waited, ears straining as the rain seemed to hurl itself harder still against the glass. Above the rain a howl shook her to the core, a howl she hadn't heard in months but she recognised it all the same. A howl which sounded like that hell hound Clarissa said belonged to a farmer was out in the storm. Jane felt a pang of pity for the beast, hell hound or not it was a brutal night to be out in. Besides, she had a soft spot for the creature, after all it had pooped in Molly's boot. Jane smiled to herself in the lamp light but the smile froze on her lips as another cry came from within the house. With a sigh and a curse, Jane hauled herself out of bed and slipped into her towelling dressing gown and put on her slippers. Then she picked up her torch and the hammer she had bought at the hardware store, whilst telling herself she might need it for the garden. She held it in her hand like a weapon as she crossed the room and opened her bedroom door, clicking on the torch. She peered into the dark corridor, just catching a tangle of black shapes fly across the long rug. Following it with her torch she found the shape hiding above the door frame of the room across from hers. Heart in her throat, Jane forced herself to look away from the shape, it was just a shape after all, and hurried down the corridor towards Mr Smithson's bedroom. She was certain the scream had come from within and she hoped she would not find him surrounded by the cloaked figures again. She reached his door and the black shadows around it scattered like speeding worms in her torch light. As she neared his door it flew open and a black figure hurtled towards her.

Chapter 15

Jane let out a startled cry as the figure swerved just in time to avoid her and the hammer that seemed to cut through the air and catch on the black fabric. She heard the fabric rip, felt the hammer pull away from her but she gripped it tightly in her hand, refusing to let it go. The figure broke away, leaving a piece of fabric clinging to the nail-pulling end as it raced down the corridor. She couldn't give chase, she couldn't move. Jane stood there, heart hammering, struggling to catch her breath as the torch shining back towards Mr Smithson's open door shook. Gasping, she waited for the rest of them to come out as she tried to listen, but the clocks drowned out any smaller sounds and Mr Smithson did not cry out again. After a while, her heart calmed down and her breathing became more normal. Jane was able to cross to the still open door and switch the light on within. There was no one there. Mr Smithson appeared asleep, snoring gently as Jane tore back all the curtains and found nothing more solid than the shadows. The only evidence that her patient had been tampered with was that his nursing bed was raised as high as possible, so that he was suspended a good five feet off the ground. She knew she hadn't left him that high. She'd looked after people who climbed over bed sides, so now she lowered all beds to the floor out of habit. She remembered doing so specifically this evening before deciding not to go to the pub. She checked his pad and repositioned him, taking care not to wake him up before lowering the bed again and slipping from the room, locking Mr Smithson's door behind her. Next, she locked her own and climbed back into bed, keeping her dressing gown on.

Tossing and turning in the big warm bed, she still couldn't sleep. First she wondered about the mysterious intruder, they had passed so fast she hadn't got a decent look at them. The odds were that it was Dora or Clarissa or Atticus, but she found it hard to believe that it actually was. After all, they had lived together and spent many hours together.

Surely she would have recognised them if it had been one of the other residents of Hacket House. Besides, she'd never seen any of them in Mr Smithson's room before. Why should she now, in the middle of the night? But if it was an outsider then how did they get into the house? It was always securely locked up by the time she stumbled home from the pub. She went most evenings after turning Mr Smithson, Clarissa turning a blind eye as long as Mr Smithson was properly cared for and Jane locked the front door again when she came home. Someone would have had to have let them in, or they must have broken in somehow. Next her thoughts moved towards Rowena and her little white coffin, the one her mum had ordered as Jane had fallen apart. Jane was ashamed how long it had been since she'd thought of her baby and her mother. Her mind had been so occupied with the house and the present, which she found far more comfortable than the atrocity of Rowena's and her mother's deaths, admittedly, but that was no excuse. Jane tossed and turned in anguish and guilt, tormenting herself. The baby's death had barrelled into her again like a ton of bricks and Jane wished she'd had the opportunity to hit *him* with a hammer, to feel his bones crack one at a time. Who knew, there was still time, when she felt stronger maybe she'd come out of hiding and let him find her. Or maybe she could find him, creep up on him one night and make him pay for what he did to Rowena and her family. Maybe she could find a way to get him to the house. Lying in the lamp light Jane heard the hell hound offer up its approval to the moon and Jane smiled a wet aching parody. She felt certain she could count on its unholy support.

She woke late at 7.30 and hurriedly dressed, rushing downstairs to the kitchen to prepare Mr Smithson's and her own breakfast.

'Good morning Jane,' said Clarissa, looking up from her morning milk and checking her watch. 'Aren't we a bit late this morning?'

'I couldn't sleep. Don't worry I got up and turned Mr Smithson at about three and checked his pad.'

'Really? There was no need, the nurses say he does not need to be turned in the night with the new bed.'

'Yeah well, I heard him crying out in the night again, so I went to check on him,' Jane continued, ignoring Clarissa's slight dig. 'Do you know what I found?'

There was an expectant pause that Jane let linger, hoping to force Clarissa to break it.

'No... what did you find?'

'Some psycho in a hood charging out of his room. He almost knocked me over.'

'Oh, you must have dreamt that. There was no one in the house last night wearing a hood.' Clarissa smiled slightly in the way that made Jane want to give her a slap.

'Really? Then why when I got up this morning was this still attached to my hammer?' Jane said, holding out the piece of thick, coarse black cloth to Clarissa.

Jane was satisfied to see the colour drain from Clarissa's face, which seemed to tighten around her red lips. For once she seemed lost for words. The toaster pinged and Jane buttered her toast then loaded everything onto a tray and pocketed her fabric, before heading for the door. At the door she turned to face Clarissa who still seemed stunned.

'Tell whoever visits Mr Smithson in the night to lower his damn bed again before leaving him unattended.'

With that Jane left the kitchen and hurried up to Mr Smithson's room.

Once Mr Smithson had eaten and drank poorly, Jane left the house again. It was only drizzling lightly. She walked past her work in the garden, then deeper into the undergrowth along the cracked path to

Atticus's shed and work room. She gathered up a load of planks of red wood from his collection, as well as a large bundle of blue tarpaulin, a hammer, and some nails, dropping them all into the squeaky wheelbarrow. It was a struggle with the mud and the broken path but eventually she managed to get it up to her garden. She set to work, digging a large hole in a spot sheltered by large gnarled trees, then burying wooden poles and hammering pieces of wood together, to the poles, and to the surrounding trees. She went inside to turn and give Mr Smithson his lunch, then returned and nailed extra wood over any cracks, creating a sort of structure with three walls and a roof. Then she nailed the tarpaulin over the wooden roof in a tight-fitting hood, hopefully making it waterproof. Then she filled in the hole covering a quarter of the structure. She hoped it would make the structure sturdier for whatever ended up using it. Tired, Jane stepped back and looked critically at what she had built. It looked a tumbledown mess but it should stay put for a bit until she could get a more permanent structure built for the animal. Looking at the clock she realised she had been working for hours. Returning the tools, Jane decided to go for a leisurely walk, criss-crossing through the undergrowth. Lost in thought, barely feeling the rain drench her, Jane slipped in the mud. As she gasped and swore, large hands reached out from the undergrowth and caught hold of her.

Chapter 16

Jane let out a startled cry and spun around. Behind her in the undergrowth, rain dripping down his face, was Atticus.

'Careful Jane.' Atticus steadied her again before letting go.

'What are you doing in there?' gasped Jane, 'You nearly scared me to death!'

'Sorry.' Atticus didn't meet her gaze. 'The cottage is back here, I was just taking a short cut.'

Jane crossed her arms over her chest and Atticus turned away.

'What's that shack for?' Atticus ran a hand through his grey hair looking back at her, she could see the sparkle in his blue eyes even as his face remained stoic.

'It's a kennel or a shelter for whatever was really howling last night,' Jane said, trying to keep her voice normal.

'Oh, that was just Farmer Jonas's dog, he mustn't like the thunder or something.'

'No, it wasn't, it wasn't even a dog… well not a normal one anyway. I know it wasn't, you know it wasn't, everyone knows it wasn't. Something weird's going on, everybody knows it. Why won't anyone admit it?' All the bottled up anger and frustration seemed to flow from Jane, her brown eyes suddenly fiery, attempted to bore into Atticus's skull as the silence rolled on and Atticus seemed to squirm.

'I hear you had quite an exchange with Clarissa this morning,' Atticus said at last.

'Yes, only because she keeps trying to say that I'm imagining things.'

A ghost of a smile flickered across his face.

'Would you like to come to the cottage? Have a drink? See how the other half live,' Atticus offered.

'It doesn't have that stench you get at the house.'

Jane looked critically at Atticus, he was the person she was closest to at the house, heck he was the closest she had gotten to a person she wasn't caring for in years. Still she wasn't sure if she could trust him. But he'd given her the only confirmation she'd had, confirmation that she was not going mad. Maybe he'd let more slip in his own home?

'Ok, but we don't go through the wilderness.'

'It's a deal,' Atticus smiled, stepping onto the cracked and broken path.

It was only wide enough to admit one person at a time, so Atticus led the way through the gnarled trees that seemed to create a canopy so thick it was practically a tunnel for them, shielding them from the rain and the sky above. Jane half expected it to turn into a giant red hole and for them to fall through it. She hoped she hadn't made a big mistake. They carried on walking, and the path became intact, before she knew it they were out of the tunnel, standing before a little white-washed wooden cottage with a thatched roof and smoke coming from the chimney. The hum of a generator was the background sound drowning out the clock at the house. A small neat garden of red tinted foliage surrounded it and Jane was enchanted, for all its simplicity it was far more attractive and homely than the grand house.

'Here we are, it's not much but it's home sweet home.' Atticus opened the painted red gate and held it for Jane.

'It's a lovely home,' Jane smiled and Atticus blushed. Atticus led the way to the front door and opened it, it was red like the gate and unlocked. Large windows made the one-room kitchen and dining room airy and bright. Atticus put the kettle on and offered Jane one of the armchairs by the small wood burner. Soon they were sat either side of it, drinking hot chocolate and making small talk like they did most evenings.

'Listen, what is going on at Hacket House?' Jane eventually blurted out. Part of her instantly regretted it at the look on Atticus's face, but she pressed on anyway.

'A lot of things have gone on at that house. I'm sure your Molly has mentioned some of the rumours and confirmed what I told you, that it's meant to be haunted.'

'Yes, and you implied that it wasn't.'

'You might not have come if you'd known. You might not have made it through the gate at all and, even then, you might not have seen anything,' Atticus said, not making eye contact.

'Why wouldn't I have made it through the gates?'

'Some people don't, they just can't stand to be on this land.'

'Why not?' Jane frowned.

'Don't know, nobody knows, it's just how it is here.' Atticus took a deep drag of hot chocolate.

'You've been drinking too much. I know you've been through a lot, but you need to cut back...'

'Yeah well you don't know the half of it. Besides it's not like there is anywhere else I can go to get away from that stench and the shadows and….'

'What shadows?' Atticus interrupted, frowning.

'The ones that dart around the walls and hide next to the clocks when they see me coming. They're more active at night. What I tried to hit last night wasn't a ghost. Nor was Dolly, nor the freaks in cloaks in Mr Smithson's room that time, and nor is whatever pooed in Molly's boot that howls in the moonlight.'

A laugh erupted from Atticus, deep in his belly, startling them both.

'No, indeed not. Listen, no one is trying to harm Mr Smithson or you but there are, well, things going on and that animal is not to be approached.' Atticus's face had recovered its former seriousness.

'What the hell is it?' Jane asked but Atticus only shook his head.

'I can't say anymore, not until it's over, but I promise you, if you wait a little longer it will all become clear.'

'I hope so.' Jane frowned unsatisfied.

'Who's Erazmus Nark?' Jane asked, accepting the biscuit Atticus offered.

'His grave is in the grounds of the house,' she explained in response to Atticus's sharp look.

'I can't find anything on him in the library or anywhere else for that matter.'

Jane could see Atticus considering his response.

'You remember I told you that my Missus used to clean at the house? Well one day in the library she discovered a secret room, pulled out the third red leather book on the second shelf and the bookcase opened.'

Chapter 17

Jane tried to spend the rest of the day as she had planned to before Atticus's revelation but it wasn't easy. As she toiled in the mud, changed Mr Smithson, and ran down to the village for dog food, she had to fight the urge to rush up to the library and find whatever was hidden in the secret room. Her trip to the village served to reinforce the urgency she felt. Today the villagers she passed turned and stared at her, stopping whatever they had previously been doing and staring at her in silence. She waved to Molly in the hairdressers but didn't stop long enough to see her wave back. As she browsed the shelves of the little pet food selection, she wondered if the garden would allow white flowers to grow. She was at the garden shop choosing and paying for the white seeds and the dog food before it occurred to her how ridiculous the thought was. Mr Owen said nothing as she paid for the dog food and seeds just bared his dentures at her like an angry dog. As she'd hurried down the street away from the shop, a figure stepped out of a doorway directly into her path so that she almost crashed into him. The uniform told her that it was the police officer Mr Hubbs.

'Watch where you're going girl or it's a trip to the station.' The large sack of meat that was Mr Hubbs smirked down at her, looking her figure up and down. Mr Hubbs stepped closer, right into Jane's space.

'We know what to do with outsiders who come here and cause trouble,' Mr Hubbs said to her cleavage.

'Sorry officer,' Jane heard someone squeak, then realised it was her own voice. She stood under Mr Hubbs' hot gaze squirming until he eventually stepped aside, allowing Jane to hurry along. Her feet took her to the deserted park she had been thinking off. She stopped at the gate and peered in. The park was still barren even when it practically beamed sunlight. Jane had wondered many times why the mothers group failed to take their toddlers on the swings there. Not today however, as she looked at the swastikas smeared on the ground and the slides in something red. Jane shuddered under the malevolent gaze of the nose-like slide; surely it had not looked as vertical before, but now it looked far too vertical to be safe. Peering at the torn bloody items of women's underwear by the swings, Jane felt the sinisterness of the place still linger and her guts turned. Turning away, she found the same group of teenagers who had greeted her on her first visit, staring at her from across the road, knowing smirks plastered to their faces.

'That will be your underwear when we've finished with you, if the house doesn't get you first,' their smirks seemed to say. Jane clutched the dog food to her chest, scurrying back to the house as the sun vacated the sky and a wind rose up, cracking the chains of the swings. As she scurried home amid the rising movement, something flapping in the wind caught her eye. Looking up, she saw it was another poster attached to a lamp post. Jane looked closer, expecting to see a blurry photograph of someone's dog. Instead, beaming up at her, was the face of a black-haired little girl. Above her head was the legend 'Missing' underneath her name, Evelyn Marsh, and Jane knew it was the little girl she had seen in the park that morning when they were going camping in the woods.

'Her bloody knickers will be in the park,' a voice whispered so close that she looked around at the staring villagers who watched her from their windows. Anger bubbling up and telling herself she would write a strongly worded complaint to the police, Jane gave the sick weirdos the finger before turning and hurrying home.

Later that day, Atticus was not at the dinner table. Jane didn't mention it and neither did Dora or Clarissa, both of whom looked far too tense. Dora talked too much, supposedly to Jane but carrying on regardless of anything Jane said, her round face stretched into an exaggerated smile. Jane felt the tension in the air as the smell pulsed around her, penetrating Dora's food and their hair and clothes. Jane did not mention her experiences in the town, nor the defilement of the park, nor Evelyn and her suspicions about the sanity of the village.

After dinner, Jane excused herself earlier than usual and turned Mr Smithson who still refused to drink or eat, instead glaring up at her with uncomfortable hatred. She was sure he'd get her if his clawed hands or contracted legs could manage it. The clocks ticked on indifferently, she'd given up shrouding them long ago. Their gaze no longer felt intrusive, but more protective and guarding. Jane left Mr Smithson howling in his bed, locked the door, and hurried to her own room where she tried to read away the hours with a torch. The hours before midnight where almost silent. The house seemed to come alive as the clock struck twelve, when heavy footfalls began to beat their rhythm along the corridor outside, creaking the floor boards and sending the shadows scampering like cockroaches. They darted across the blankets she lay under and over the pages of her book, down towards the dark at the bottom of her bed with her feet.

Once the traffic had died down, shortly after the clocks struck two, Jane switched off her torch and clambered out of bed, still in her day clothes, and slipped on her trainers. Grabbing the hammer and torch she exited the room and hurried along the corridor. Jane made her way around the clocks, down corridors and up the crooked staircase leading to the library. She reached the door as the dog howled, so close that it could well be in the house with them. She ignored it and hurried inside, switching on the light. The secret room was exactly where Atticus said it would be. When Jane had pulled out the leather book, the whole shelving unit had creaked and groaned to one side, just enough for Jane to see into the black hole. She held her breath and strained her hearing, wondering how the hell had no one heard that dreadful grinding sound? Surely they'd come running to see what had caused it? A roar erupted from somewhere nearby and Jane jumped backwards, banging against the desk. Cursing under the disapproving gaze of a particularly nasty looking grandfather clock, Jane tried to listen again. It wasn't easy with the hammering of her heart but there were no pounding footsteps heading towards the library. No, this section of the house seemed to be devoid of human activity.

Half expecting to find a face peering out at her, Jane lifted up the torch with a trembling hand and peered more closely into the crevice. The darkness seemed to run for cover under its glare. It too appeared to be filled with books. Apprehension held her in place. Maybe she should go back to her room and pretend the smells and shadows weren't there, like Dora and Clarissa did. After all, they weren't harming anyone. Perhaps she should robotically care for Mr Smithson and the garden until she had enough money to go backpacking somewhere hot and humid with long bright days and no shadows. Some paradise without deserted parks and villages brewing violence. Looking into what felt like the rabbit hole she had half expected to come across all her life, she was tempted. Even so, curiosity and a determination to see this thing through, as well as a curious love and affinity she had developed for the monstrous house, its wild garden and the animal she had left dog food out for, nailed her feet to the floor. Intuition told her that if she went rooting through the secret room she'd fall slap bang into the mystery of the house and never find her way out again. With nothing really to lose, Jane hesitantly slid into the secret room.

Chapter 18

Once in the room she was able to see it properly. The entire room was far cleaner and less uninhabited than she had expected. Instead of being caked in a thick layer of dust the desk, the armchair behind it, as well as the books on the shelves surrounding the little room were devoid of dust and Jane was sure someone must be cleaning it regularly. The desk, really too big for the space, left just enough room for an equally clean ladder so that someone thin would be able to examine the higher shelves.

This isn't part of the house, I really have fallen down the rabbit hole, Jane thought, as she searched for the obligatory clock and the walls seemed to close in around her. There was no clock, but there *was* something very wrong here. A large old piece of paper was laid out on the desk, yellowed and faded with age, clearly left out for her to find. It was the dustiest thing in the room, in fact she could see fingerprints in the dust at the edge of the parchment. Jane had to blow off the dust to read the writing. Finding that wasn't quite enough, she used her sleeve to wipe it off and found herself staring at a map of some sort. She peered closely at the intricate ink drawing that seemed to point out certain trees with Hacket House slap bang in the centre and the 'mistress's cottage' to the right. Jane thought she recognised some of the trees indicated, as well as the various paths and roads in the grounds. But there was something else indicated by a series of intricate web-like lines that criss-crossed the parchment. Jane had no idea what they meant but upon seeing the name and date in the bottom right hand corner she was very glad she hadn't picked it up. Erazmus Nark 18… then under it in similar writing, the same name Erazmus Nark 2011. A cold shiver ran down Jane's back as she read the name Nark and she drew away, no longer willing to touch the map. She used the beam of the torch to examine the parchment. Parts of the intricate web that crisscrossed the map looked fresher than others as if the second Nark, a distant relative perhaps, had added them to the map. Intrigued, Jane searched the corners of the map for a key of some sort. She found it in a corner, faded with age and clearly in the earlier Nark's writing. Next to a small sample of the web-like lines was the inscription 'The Path of the Beast.' Suddenly it seemed very cold in her book-lined tomb. Swallowing her growing sense of panic, she gritted her teeth and carried on. Finding nothing else of interest on the map she examined the desk drawers. Three she found to be empty after prising them open, the last one flew open as if it had been waiting for her. It was filled with a mixture of thick ancient parchment paper, crumpled and torn and definitely not written in Nark's hand, and thinner, recognisable paper handwritten on by Nark. The older papers contained mainly diagrams and verses that appeared to be torn from older books she suspected were written in Latin, Nark having written the translations besides the verses he considered worth translating. Most were blasphemous, describing evil forces at the expense of God, and some appeared to be spells of some sort. The drawings depicted beasts of such grotesque appearance, their limbs so twisted and mismatched that Jane could have guessed that the creatures were man made and comprised of many different animal parts, including human heads, body parts and organs. She found she could not look too closely at the monstrosities Nark described as fiends. Among the drawings she found hideous illustrations of trees, coming to life, tearing their roots from the earth, whipping their branches back as people fled before them. Their bark was knotted and twisted and with a shudder Jane was reminded of her beloved garden.

Nark's personal papers seemed to be documenting the noises of the house, the shadows that darted across the walls, the trees he was convinced followed him when he took a turn in the garden. He wrote about the monstrosities that he believed haunted him both in his sleep and when he left the house. How he was convinced that the land was alive, and blood-soaked, that its influence ran through the surrounding area and was responsible for many local atrocities and the occasional madness of the entire village of Bramley. That it had magical powers to prolong life indefinitely. He wrote of his determination to explore and harness the power of the land, to cling onto the land and force it to do his bidding. How he experimented by planting different plants in the land or burying different items in the dirt. Every so often he would reference a book that Jane would painstakingly look up on the bookshelves, only to discover a fresh abomination. Most of the books seemed to be collected by something called the Church of Hacket, a series of handwritten tomes, written in red ink by various people describing the destruction of the village church Molly had told her about, as well as many other supposed incidents going back as far as the Vikings. Jane knew she'd be having nightmares for weeks as she dug deeper into rumours of insanity, massacres, rape and necrophilia. From the ground opening up to swallow invading armies and missionaries, to cannibalism during the Black Death, the list of atrocities and madness went on. She thought she heard the house growl around her as she read on, unable to take her eyes away from the terrible red words detailing what the Church of Hacket claimed had happened in the area. They kept on going, with more recent ones describing Dolly Hacket, the founder of the Church of Hacket, supposedly sacrificing some of her many children to the land, and the disappearance of her husband James Hacket, who built Hacket House. Dolly was also the author the first two tomes, one monster of a book dedicated to as much history and hearsay as she could unearth. In the second one, completed by another church member, Dolly wrote about the voice of the land and the sacrifices it asked her to make. The mention of the pain she felt having to sacrifice her children cut deep into Jane. Far deeper than the woman's clearly insane ramblings. The books carried on, some historical, while others documented the present. Some of the more recent books had pages torn away. Some of the remaining pages claimed the land had possessed the house's maintenance man, driving him to smash his pregnant wife's skull in until she had to be identified by dental records. The husband was therefore spared from an unhappy marriage and the land had another sacrifice. She was apparently buried in Hacket House's graveyard. The most recent volume was begun a mere three years ago and remained barely started. To Jane's horror, the latest entry was dated just the other night. Brilliant scarlet leapt from the page, graphically describing the men of the village dragging their wives and daughters to the deserted park and violating them as the rain poured down and the thunder tore through the sky, the blood flowing freely.

'Screams of pain and lust mingled in the air, combining into one unified primeval scream.'

Jane felt sick, worse she felt dizzy, and she swore never to go down to the village again because she felt it was true. But she had to keep reading.

Next, she started on a file of newspaper clippings, dating from the nineteenth to the early twentieth century, all of which described the murder of various women, most of whom were described as prostitutes. Three had lived within the slums of London, ten others had lived within twenty miles of the house, all had been discovered badly mutilated. Their heads and organs had been separated from their bodies and exhibited as far as two miles away from the rest of their remains. Mary Brown's intestines had even been used to decorate the gate of Hacket House. Jane's stomach turned again; reading about what she expected were Nark's crimes was just as bad as reading myths and hype about what had supposedly happened in the surrounding area. The newspaper cuttings were starkly real and for the first time she felt a rush of real hatred for the man.

At the very bottom of the drawer, under the papers and the newspaper clippings, was one final yellowed piece of paper. With a sense of foreboding she couldn't explain, Jane reached down and plucked out the paper, holding it to her light. The weight of the room bore down on her as she read the only two words on the back - Faith Hope. Jane turned the paper over and discover that it was in fact an old black and white photograph. Jane stared at it. It had to be some trick of the light surely? The woman with the long dark hair was about forty, completely naked with her legs wide open, pointing towards the camera. The head of a snake, far too large to have any business being down there, was emerging from her vagina as if the rest of it was coiled up deep inside her. The woman's sunken eyes bore into her as if she could see Jane and the contemptuous sneer on her lips was directed straight at her. Jane's phone rang and, heart pounding, Jane dropped the photo and tried to compose herself. Reaching into her pocket she extracted the out of place metal device and, more to shut it up than anything else, answered it.

Chapter 19

Hand trembling, Jane held it to her ear and a voice she wasn't sure was her own croaked out a 'Hello?' There was nothing at the end of the phone for a moment except breathing. She hadn't received a phone call since she'd moved to Hacket House, and now some creep had her number. Jane thought of Nark and the woman in the photograph and her blood ran cold.

'Who is this?' Jane was pleased to recognise her own voice again, even as a fiend roared in the distance. Having read Nark's papers, she was certain whatever had pooped in Molly's shoe and howled in the night was one of the fiends Nark had tried to catch. More heavy breathing greeted her, but she found some comfort in the familiar roar. Jane was just about to hang up when a voice finally spoke, and it was far worse than some monster from beyond the grave.

'Marnie, it's me.'

Jane screamed and hurled the device away. It bounced off the thick books and clattered to the floor. Jane did not see this as she had hurtled from the little room, seconds before her phone hit the ground. Her legs propelled her down endless long corridors, her mind nothing more than a white-hot mass of panic. Somehow, she found herself in her bedroom, panting and staring at her reflection in the big mirror as if she did not recognise the woman standing before her. The former love of her life, the murderer of their child, had found her. She should be hurling her shit into her suitcase and abandoning the house and the life she had built. She should be running to the train station and disappearing into what was left of the night. Instead she just stood staring at the woman in the mirror, the woman with big, dark, wild eyes and black hair, her permanently dark skin looking waxy and yellow-tinged as if she was sick. The red hoodie and comfortable sweatpants she wore were also alien to her, as if they'd been put on by a different woman. A woman who'd never made love to a child killer. Was that really what she looked like now? Somehow, not looking like Richard's wife, helped calm her and the panic started to fade. Her little wooden clock struck the hour as an unnatural calm descended into Jane. She was no longer his wife Marnie. Thoughtfully she crossed the room and locked the door, sending the shadows scattering in her path. The papers mentioned the need for sacrifice; she hadn't believed them but that didn't matter now. Let Richard come for Marnie if he dared. As if hearing her thoughts, the fiend outside howled again.

Jane slept far better than she felt she had any right to. After a couple of hours of white rabbits, becoming ten feet tall, and stomping around under even bigger red mushrooms, crushing anything in her path. She woke up and cared for Mr Smithson. The old man smelt far worse than anything she'd ever smelt before and he seemed exhausted. He was far too tired to eat or drink.

'Mr Smithson stinks today. And he wouldn't eat or drink. He was so tired he just kept snoring at me,' Jane heard herself say to Clarissa over her newspaper at the breakfast bar.

'It is time for Mr Smithson's bath, I have arranged for an agency carer to come over at ten to help you bathe him. Please check that the ceiling hoist is charged and run the bath water,' Clarissa said in a bored, tired voice without looking up.

It was clear someone else had had a bad night. Wondering why Clarissa had not informed her before, Jane went out into the garden and stood in the crisp cold, sniffing the fresh air and looking around. From her barren land to the wilderness of the garden beyond, everything seemed normal and comforting and Jane knew that Richard was not on the land of Hacket House. Half convinced that the phone call had just been a particularly nasty nightmare, Jane went to her makeshift shelter and peered inside. *Had she really dug down that deep?* she asked herself, knowing but afraid to admit that the six foot deep pit was not of her own construction. It was more a grave than anything else really. Jane shivered, peering into the gloom and half expecting something to be looking back at her.

A man lay stretched out in the bottom of the grave. Naked except for the evil symbols carved deep into his flesh, his throat cut to the bone creating a second mouth. The two scarlet pits where his eyes should be gaped back at her accusingly. The bloody roses around the sockets spoke to Jane.

'I was alive when they did this to me Jane,' they seemed to say.

The mouth remained silent, hung open in a soundless scream, exposing two lines of rotten cracked teeth, while a halo of granite hair, alive with bugs and worms, framed his head. The skin was grey and sunken in deeply at the cheeks, bringing the shape of the skull beneath into sharp focus. Jane let out a strangled cry and reversed away so fast that she found herself sprawled on her back, winded, her heart hammering.

'Are you alright Jane?' Atticus stood over her, his face lined with concern, holding out a grubby hand.

Stunned, Jane just stared back at him, her tongue feeling too heavy and cumbersome to speak. Silently she raised a shaking hand and pointed towards the shelter. Atticus followed her finger then looked back at Jane. His face was unreadable, but Jane had the distinct impression that he was hesitating, reluctant to go and look. Jane cautiously pulled herself to her feet using Atticus's arm to steady herself and wordlessly they looked at each other. Suddenly, as if making up his mind, Atticus turned from Jane and strode to the hole, peering inside. For a long moment he remained bent down staring, into the shelter, and Jane wondered what kind of sadistic serial killer was on the loose.

'There's nothing there, just dirt. Well, and an empty dog bowl and the biggest turd you've ever seen.' Atticus's voice was tight and forced. All Jane could do was stare wordlessly back at him.

'What did you see, love?' He never called her love, or anything else for that matter, always Jane.

'He… it was a man,' Jane eventually blurted out and her mouth felt like it had been stuffed with cotton wool.

'He was dead, cut up badly, no eyes, see no evil.' Jane sobbed the last words out and Atticus crossed over to her and held her as she sobbed onto his jacket.

Still shaken, but slightly calmer after a shot or two of Atticus's whisky, Jane ran back into the house at 9.50. As she stepped into the hall a million tiny shadows scarpered across the walls and ceiling as if they had been awaiting her return. Jane ignored them as she hurried up to Mr Smithson's room, deliberately not looking at the wailing figure in the bed, and started running the boat-like high tech bath. It was a ceiling tract hoist, the top concealed in a cupboard, the end and the remote tucked away conveniently behind one of the less malevolent looking clocks that resided in the bathroom. Far more convenient and less common than the large cranes that struggle on carpet and which Jane knew are also used to shift engines. Mr Smithson wailed and Jane tugged the hook end towards her, and trying the remote. Luckily, the cord took the hook end up.

As she was playing with the hoist something drew her eyes towards the window. A strange feeling came over her, as if the room and the clocks were vibrating. Shadows scuttled for cover and chains rattled, something mechanical somewhere deep down rumbled, and Jane half closed her eyes and staggered towards the window, looking out into the surrounding area below. Gasping for breath, she looked down, not immediately down at the shaking structure, she had no stomach for that, but at the area around the house. She was certain she'd see something extraordinary, like trees uprooting, tearing themselves from the earth and wandering from the garden in a way that said they would no longer tolerate being in Hacket House's garden a moment longer. Or the inhabitants of the graves clawing themselves out of the earth and descending on the house. A cold chill infected first her flesh, then her bones as she thought of Nark. If any of them would come, it would be him, surely. Scanning the area, Jane was half relieved, half disappointed to see that nothing so dramatic was happening and the trees remained in their positions, the graves undisturbed. The only noticeable change was a car outside the main gate, someone in purple crouched, doubled over beside the bushes next to the road. The earth seemed to stand still again, and the house fell silent.

'The carer is not coming.' Jane spun around to find Clarissa stood in the doorway, dressed in a business suit and towering heels.

'She's been overcome by food poisoning.' Clarissa rolled her eyes and pushed up her sleeves. 'I will assist you to bathe Mr Smithson.'

It took them an hour and Mr Smithson screamed like a vampire in the sunlight under the gaze of the wonky totem pole of a clock. Standing directly over the bath, the clock looked hideously out of place in the modern bathroom. Jane was surprised how competent a carer Clarissa was and swore to seek further assistance in future as the clocks looked hungrily on. Jane felt sure they were hungry like the fiend outside. They hoisted Mr Smithson back to bed, dried him, and were relieved to find that he had not pooed in the sling. Jane went to the chest of drawers, dodging around the large malevolent clock she was sure had been moved. Turning around, a white vest clutched in her hand, Jane was shocked to see Clarissa's hand squeezing Mr Smithson's claw as she seemed to bend over him. As Jane got closer, Clarissa let go of Mr Smithson's hand and moved away from him as if nothing had happened. As they put the vest on Mr Smithson, Clarissa was oddly silent and refused to meet Jane's eye.

Jane left Mr Smithson drinking with Clarissa. He had refused to drink for her so Jane left them to it, returning to her room and getting her coat before heading down to the garden and off into Bramley. She did not want to step foot in the village again, but from there she could catch one of the infrequent buses to a larger town nearby and find a phone shop. She needn't have worried. The village of Bramley was deserted, all the blinds and shops were closed, and in some cases boarded up, as if the entire village had disappeared in the night. All that remained was the racist graffiti and old crusty underwear in the park, along with a missing pet and child posters on each lamp post. Totally alone, Jane waited at the bus stop, the desertedness weighing down on her and thought of the blonde baby she'd seen in the bakery with the mothers group. She hadn't seen her since. As twenty minutes ticked by and still nobody stirred, a dread she couldn't explain seemed to settle. Maybe her first instinct to kidnap the baby and take her away from this place had been right after all. The bus arrived and took her to a cheery picturesque town where the people seemed normal and minded their own business. She bought a new phone and a new sim that came with a new number. She had left her phone on the floor in the secret room and had no intention of retrieving it.. Thank god she'd backed up all her photos. Then she looked around the shops and savoured being in a normal place were things were ordinary, a place where the people didn't stare at her and the land wasn't alive with some force she couldn't explain. Where she could tell herself, at least pretend, that there were no ghosts and no shadows that legged it when she saw them. It was a long wait for the bus home and, as she stood at the empty bus stop, she wondered about not going back, leaving all her possessions and whatever fiends howled in the night and brought her mutilated ghosts. If she did that Richard would definitely not be able to find her. But she'd be alone again, utterly alone. So when the bus pulled up and all the people got off, she got on board and started the journey back towards Bramley. The village was just as she'd left it a few hours before. Uneasy, Jane went to Molly's house and found it as barren as every other house in the village. Molly's car was dumped haphazardly on the road outside. Posting her new number through the door, Jane turned and hurried off towards her own house.

Chapter 20

For the next few weeks the world, at least for Jane, developed the quality of a surrealist dream. Now that she'd given up the pub and drinking, her old problems returned. At night she would lie awake, trying to make sense of the ghost in the grave as the shadows skittered across the ceiling. They were no longer hiding from her but rejoicing and partying in her presence. Eventually the ticking of Sue, her own delicate and benevolent clock, who was now her night-time companion, lulled her to sleep with her gentle ticking. Every night something laid beside her in the darkness and she sensed its weight on the bed, even when she thought she was awake. Its presence never moved to touch her, nor her it, for if she felt someone beside her, then she'd have to deal with them. If she couldn't feel them, she wouldn't have to face them. She couldn't see them, even with the lights on, only the weight beside her betrayed their presence. She no longer changed her clothes in the bedroom, nor did she ever sleep naked anymore.

Some nights she'd jump awake to find herself surrounded by dark figures. After the third night it happened, she realised they were giant red clocks with looming black shadows that barred her exit from the room as people, lots of them, dashed past her bedroom door. People raced along the corridor every night now, creaking the floorboards as if the house was a musical instrument. From the hours of one to two, she'd wake up to the playing of the floorboards, and on the occasions when she was unguarded she would stumble into the corridor in her pyjamas. Jane would find herself surrounded by the population of the village wearing their robes with their hoods pulled down to mask their faces, walking around her with nods of acknowledgement, before evaporating into the darkness again. Some nights she'd try to catch one or two people who'd just mumble something and skirt past her, leaving her struggling to swim in the sea of people until she found herself safely in her own room. She'd lock the door and curl up, relieved to be in her own bed. Her hammer never left her side on these nights, as she wondered which hood Mr Hubbs' leering face was underneath. The traffic only went one way, towards Mr Smithson's room. By morning she'd convince herself that she'd dreamt it yet again, that the bags under Clarissa's eyes were just coincidence, and the gleam in Dora's eye was because of the upcoming yarn festival and nothing else. Then the night would play out again and Jane would not be sure what was real and what was not.

The only thing that seemed real these days was her garden; The damp red soil and the chill in the air as she and Atticus planted walks and fence posts and installed a proper, giant kennel built from some planks left over from the clock-making frenzy. Even her garden was not safe from the dream world that threatened to consume her. She would see figures in the distance, blurred human forms and larger figures of creatures long dead and *extinct*. Sometimes she'd try to approach one of the more human forms, but no matter how fast she ran towards them they would disappear, merging into the land or the red trees before she reached their spot.

She would also see movements in the trees, even on days with no wind, as if someone was up in the branches moving them around. When she went to check, poking with a long stick, she'd find the tree empty and barren and wonder again if she was going insane.

One night she woke with a gasp and immediately her mouth filled with wet dirt. It was everywhere, up her nose, in her ears, clinging to her eyes, under her clawing fingers. The cold seeped through her clothes, then into her flesh and bones. She tried to scream but an avalanche of dirt caused her to choke. Panic tore at her and she tried to scream again with the same effect, swallowing the dark, tainted earth as thoughts of human sacrifice played a loop through her mind along with the stories of village madness she'd read and dreamt about. Somewhere above, despite the dirt and the worms she felt creeping over her flesh and investigating her ears, she heard voices and sounds. Singing, or chanting more likely. Her desperate fingers clawed the earth as she held her breath and prayed. Prayed that now was not her time to join Rowena in the earth. Despite everything, she wanted to live, to carry on, to punish Richard and live on for both of them. They couldn't end like this, if she died all trace of Rowena would too and no crazy village was going to do that. No fucking way!

As she clawed, the world and her thoughts began to fade as she felt herself weaken and start the slow descent into unconsciousness and certain death. Her hands became more and more free. The biting air that assaulting them drove her on to free her arms, and finally her mouth and nose, coughing, spluttering, and half screaming into the night air. Her throat burnt on the red damp earth especially as it rose up along with her bile and last night's dinner. The chanting got louder as an image of the man with no eyes reared its ugly head. She felt a strong hand seize the back of her hair and yank her back, as if trying to pull her into the earth. Something dreadful howled, far too close for comfort as Jane's bladder emptied and her entire body began to thrash and rive, fighting the earth and whatever wished to drag her back into it. Her scalp burned as her hair and bits of skin tore off in the man's fist. By now the chanting was no longer just a sound, oh no, it pulsed through the earth which seemed to beat out a steady rhythm, not dissimilar to the chiming of the clocks. Soon it pulsed through her body as, somewhere nearby, above the chanting, her song White Rabbit played. As the grip loosened, Jane sat up and found herself surrounded by the villagers who were shrouded by their cloaks. Then the world went completely black and she was under the earth once more, dirt in her nose and mouth. A cold lifeless weight on her chest pushed her down and Jane screamed again.

This time she woke up, freezing cold, and disorientated. She spat out a load of dirt and coughed. Her scalp burnt as she sat up, brushing it against the pillow someone had put behind her head. Sitting up, Jane found herself soaked but beside a roaring fire. After some further looking around, she realized that someone had put a sheet on her sofa and laid her out on top of it. Switching on the lamp nearby, the one she used to use for reading, Jane saw that mud clung to her hands and pyjamas. In the bathroom, as the shower warmed up over the white porcelain bath, Jane scrubbed the mud from her hands. Seeing the earth caked under her nails brought everything up to her throat. Mud and Dora's casserole burst from her mouth again, spraying into the sink until the rust coloured fluid became green and Jane had nothing else to give. Shakily, and not convinced that she would not pass out, Jane stepped into the bath and under the shower, still wearing her pyjamas. Once the dirt was out of her hair, she removed her pyjamas and took a long hot bath, relaxing as the water sucked the cold from her flesh and bones.

The next morning Jane found herself in her own bed, clean, warm and safe as if nothing had happened. Only the ache in her throat and scalp told her otherwise.

Every day Jane waited for the dreaded phone call. She found that turning it on silent helped, but every time she looked at the little screen her heart skipped a beat. She knew she'd get the call again and she couldn't shake the gut feeling that her past and present were about to collide.

As the nights grew darker and Atticus spent more evenings alone in his cabin, Jane found herself talking to Clarissa more. Clarissa actually seemed to be eating instead of picking at her meals or just drinking wine, milk and coffee. After dinner they'd sit together and make small talk. Clarissa seemed happier, smiling more and even laughing upon occasion, throwing her bright red hair back and emitting hearty laughter that Jane would have never thought her capable of. The three women would talk and laugh over Dora's women's magazines and Jane appreciated the change of atmosphere.

One night, such as many others, as Dora read another celebrity diet, Jane excused herself and went upstairs to turn the now increasingly declining Mr Smithson. He was becoming so much like a corpse, a twisted ancient mummy trapped in a state of perpetual silent screaming that Jane could hardly bear to touch him, even with the gloves. Luckily, the clocks seemed to sympathise. Having repositioned him, she tried to give him a drink as normal, spooning the thickened gloop in, only for him to not swallow it. Jane felt her pocket vibrate. With a trembling hand she took the phone out and looked at it. She didn't recognise the number and hesitated, staring down at the screen along with the nearest clock. Unable to bear the suspense a moment longer, Jane pressed the green button and held it to her ear.

'Marnie? Is that you?' said a familiar voice down the other end.

Chapter 21

'Marnie? It's me, Claire, are you there?'

'Listen I… we really missed you when you left.'

In the pause that followed, Jane listened to Claire's breathing and mumbling to someone else in the background. Claire had been her best friend in junior then secondary school. They'd only grown apart after Claire went on a gap year straight after school. She'd cried for days at losing her best friend. Now, after not hearing from her since Rowena's murder, she couldn't bring herself to utter a peep.

'Listen, I'm really sorry about what happened to Rowena and for, well, it's so hard to know what to say after something so terrible happens.' There was another long pause as Jane rolled her eyes at the nearest clock..

'Still, it was really good to see you online again, to see that you've finally moved on and are living in such a beautiful house.'

'What do you mean you saw me online?' Jane barely recognised the croak as her own voice. The clocks leaned forwards and Jane sensed their interest in the unfolding human drama.

'Marnie! It's so good to hear your voice again. I saw your profile online and your number and I thought I just had to give you a ring and congratulate you on making up with Richard. It's so big of you to forgive…'

Jane hung up, heart pounding. Quickly she looked on the social network they'd always used and typed her married name, Marnie Daniels, into the search engine. To her horror, one of the pictures Molly took on their camping trip was her profile picture. Scrolling down her horror only grew as she realised that the profile, though not completely public, included Hacket House as her address and the new telephone number hardly anyone had. It was clear that Molly and others had betrayed her but what had really dug the knife in was putting her down as being in a relationship with Richard.

Running down the now familiar corridors, Jane had no idea where she should go or what she should do, but she had to do something. Richard would be coming, with his handsome face and empty words, demanding she and the world forgive him and forget Rowena ever existed! Fuck that! His pretty boy face and charm might fool the world, but it would not fool her and it would not fool Hacket House. She took the long way round and reached her room, flinging open the door. Within seconds she had found what she was looking for and was once again hurtling down the corridor, this time it was her rocking and riding the floorboards. The irony was not lost on her as she dashed down the stairs so fast she could be falling, and found herself bursting through the little doorway of the cosy room where the household spent their evenings.

Both Dora and Clarissa sat together on the over-sized sofa amidst a sea of knitting wool.

'Jane, what's wrong?' Dora cooed, forgetting her wool and standing up, sending it tumbling to the floor. 'You look like you've seen a ghost!'

'Jane, put down the hammer and we can talk about whatever's upset you.' Clarissa's words sent red sparks before Jane's eyes. How dare she sound so calm!

'Richard is coming, and you sent him here, you and Molly and your crazy little village. Now you're going to help me kill him and feed him to whatever walks this land.'

'Jane…'

'Don't you dare call me Jane!'

'Marnie, we can explain, and we will help you. We want Richard too.' Clarissa stood up and Jane was reminded of the Red Queen, so majestic were her movements. What happened next happened so fast Jane barely had time to register it. Suddenly the motherly but large Dora was upon her, the sweet tang of something in her mouth and nose as the world began to slip away and the hammer dropped from her limp fingers.

Chapter 22

'Marnie! Marnie! Wake up! You have to help me!' Richard's voice cut through the fog of unconsciousness. He sounded frightened, genuinely frightened, and nothing ever used to scare him. If he was pleading with her, he must be really desperate. Reluctantly, Jane opened her eyes and found herself staring straight into the slack, corpse-like face of Mr Smithson. With a scream she squirmed and thrashed and discovered that her hands were tied to Mr Smithson's nursing bed. Worse still, she was lying in the single bed inches away from him. A guttural roar emitted from Mr Smithson's gaping mouth and the stench of decay and the ominous dampness of the sheet, followed by the acidic tang of urine, hit her even as she shuffled as far from Mr Smithson as possible in the tiny space. Unable to escape the smell of piss and the scent of decay on his breath she gagged and gasped.

'Marn! Tell them to let me go, that I haven't done anything.'

Looking up, Jane half expected to see Richard, suspended over them on some sort of medieval torture device. Jane did a double take; all around the bed, craning over it at angles no inanimate object should be able to manage without hinges or extreme violence, were Mr Smithson's grandfather clocks. She saw them move, heard the creaking and cracking of the red wood as they bent their heads so that the clock faces loomed before them. The sound of the creaking set her teeth on edge and she felt naked and terribly exposed under the gleaming faces. To her right, closest to Mr Smithson's face, was the malevolent one, tonight his intricate carvings looked like savage sharpened horns, the patterns of the bark looked like a combination of nasty scars and prison tattoos. His clock face twisted as if melted, his hands like sharp tiny knives seemed to glare. Someone activated the bed and Jane and Mr Smithson were forced to sit up together and look out.

The hooded figures surrounded them on every side. They stood motionless, ignoring Richard's whining. She now saw that he was tied to a large padded chair on wheels that Mr Smithson had once used. Standing beside him, was Dora's relative Dolly. Her face was twisted in a rotten grin, her head cocked to one side as she smiled at Mr Smithson. Still Richard called out to her but Jane barely noticed him. Compared to Dolly, who looked like an unmoving living nightmare, and The Red Queen who had just emerged from behind the clocks which had cleared a path for her, he really was insignificant. The hooded figures all turned as one to face her, only Dolly remained staring at Mr Smithson, a black tongue emerging from her mouth and flicking over her dry carnivorous lips. Through her growing terror and panic Jane kicked herself, why had she not seen it before? Dolly did not need help, she was a part of the house and land like the dead man in the grave. She was Dolly Hacket, the child murderer and cult leader.

The Red Queen stood dressed head to toe in blood red, with her hair spiked and twisted around a red wood structure forming a wild red crown, sharp like thorns. The Red Queen was Clarissa and she stood before her, glaring at her with more hatred than Jane had ever seen before.

The Red Queen wants my head, Jane thought, and she continued to thrash.

'Ladies and gentlemen!' A voice came from Clarissa that Jane barely recognised. It was harsh and sharp and tinkled like shattering glass.

'Most of you know why we are gathered here tonight. However, there are three of us here who do not know why we are here and have a right to know. The reason we are here is because of Erazmus Nark.' The fiend which Jane knew had a lot of teeth howled outside the window. It was so close it would have to be somehow perched on the window ledge.

'Three years ago, myself and my dear husband Colin came to Hacket House to stay with Colin's senile father. What we found was an elderly man, half mad and raving, violent and cruel, who had been diagnosed with dementia. A dying man. My Colin, however, found something far worse. That the old man was not his father, but totally and utterly possessed by an Erazmus Nark. Nark had come to Hacket House in life to investigate the land the house is built on and harness its power for his own evil ends. As the land became more volatile towards him, Nark used black magic and was able to leave his human body and possess the body of his host. An elderly man called Julian Hacket, a direct descendent of Dolly and Arthur Hacket. He remained within Hacket until he died and then, with no other living person to possess, he cowered in the corpse. That is until this land, in a fury, shook so violently that it forced Nark from his host, upon which he was absorbed by the land. Somehow, after many years, he managed to escape the clutches of the land and take over Tobias Smithson's body. I believe he gained possession of the old man a mere two years before his death and, like before when the old man died, whatever foulness passes for Erazmus Nark's soul took possession of my Colin. To contain Nark, we were forced to turn my Colin from a handsome young man with all his future before him into that decrepit, barely alive monster on the bed. The church and I keep his form twisted and crippled and confined to keep Nark from doing any further harm. But we are here tonight to enact the sacrifice necessary to rid my Colin of the abomination that is Erazmus Nark and give Erazmus to the land that both feeds us and feeds from us.' The old man she had cared for over many hours and months howled like a tortured animal and attempted to move his contracted limbs. It was as if he heard and understood Clarissa's words.

'Just as you read about in your books, we will do to you,' Clarissa practically screamed, a mad glint in her eye.

'You're crazy, you're completely nuts. You'll never get away with this you know,' Richard whined and Jane noticed the bloody gash on his forehead for the first time.

I hope that hurt, Jane thought, glaring at him. What had she ever seen in this whiner? Anyone would think he was covered in piss and trussed up close to the supposed possessed monster whose inhuman breath made her guts turn.

'Oh shut up you pathetic little man,' Clarissa roared and Richard obeyed, it was the type of command you disobeyed at your own peril.

Jane watched Clarissa take a deep breath and visibly control herself before turning and addressing the gathered congregation.

'Now I know some of you felt the need to find an external sacrifice was unnecessary. That Atticus Whiteley would do, after the murder of his wife who was three months pregnant at the time.'

Jane saw some of the hooded figures nod.

'But contrary to some people's belief, the dark writings I have had translated do not recognise a fetus as a living child. Such rituals carried out in other parts of the world on mothers who have aborted their babies have been disastrous. As this land is your God, I strongly suggest you accept the dark guidance.' With a withering look, Clarissa turned to Richard.

'You are here because you smashed your baby daughter to pieces rather than be a man and handle fatherhood whilst your wife worked nights to pay the mortgage. You could always twist your Marnie around your little finger, couldn't you? Do you remember at the inquest? When they said your daughter had injuries similar to being in a car accident? What a waste, and for what? So your wife would make more of a fuss of you, have the energy to fuck you more often?' The Red Queen was up in his face now, growling at him, and the only other sounds were the ticking of the clocks and someone sobbing. With a start, Jane realised it was her.

'You were a bitch to catch.' Jane was shocked to hear Molly's voice as a hooded figure stepped forwards. 'Totally incompetent, worst tinder date ever. What was it? Once you missed the train. Then you had to work late when you were meant to meet us and the fiend known as the hell hound at the campsite. That's what he told me, but I later found out he'd pulled some woman at a pub and ended up bonking her all night. Then, when he was meant to meet us in the pub the next day, you know what this stupid fucker did? Went to the wrong Bramley, a hundred fucking miles away.' Jane saw her count down on her fingers. 'Then I knew I'd have to pull some clever shit to catch him. I…'

'THANKYOU, Molly.' Molly looked at Clarissa for a moment then stepped back. Jane knew she was glaring under the hood.

'We knew you'd come here to get your Marnie back, the ritual requires the presence of both parents, either living or dead. Besides, this land is always hungry, who knows whom it may take. Sometimes when this ritual is carried out both parents are required,' Clarissa continued.

The walls of the room began to throb and pulse and The Red Queen stepped away from Richard, leading the hooded figures in a chant Jane could barely hear as both the old man and the fiend on the window ledge howled. As the walls beat their own rhythm, Jane thought of Rowena and watched Richard fight the straps holding him in place. She had to get out of this, to keep going for her daughter. She was so engrossed in her own thoughts and fear that she barely registered the metamorphosis before her eyes until it was too late, and it was her turn to thrash and scream in terror again. Where the six clocks had been was now one giant wooden monster, twisted beyond belief, wooden spikes jutting out in every direction. It resembled a tree in that it was wood but that was all. Tentacles streamed out and helped it climb onto the bed and hold itself over her and Mr Smithson. It had no eyes or face to speak of, just a hole with jagged wooden teeth that it ground and cracked making a sound not dissimilar to a chainsaw. As it bore down on the bed Jane closed her eyes and prayed.

Chapter 23

Suddenly her thrashing arms were free as if something had been cut. Quickly, amidst a horrific screeching sound she found to be her own screams, she scrambled away from Mr Smithson and the wooden animal. It came so close as it loomed over them that her clothes, and in places her skin, snagged against the creature's spikes creating long grooves in her flesh and wrenching fresh screams from her. Without looking back she swung her arms and head over the bed rails. Her body, legs and feet followed, but they didn't even touch the ground before creaking wood and bone tentacles seized her under the arms and lifted her into the air. Pain shot through her shoulders and a part of her wondered about dislocation even as the creature tossed her into the air. The air that suddenly stank of decay and freshly dug earth. The creature caught her and held her in its tentacles so that she was forced to face Mr Smithson and bear down on the now visibly grey and rotting figure along with the creature. To her horror she saw the old man's face, gaping toothlessly up at her, begin to crumble and collapse in on itself. The milky blue eyes expanded and popped in their sockets. Blood and gloop ran down what remained of his grey cheeks as something deeper cracked and popped within his chest. Jane, beginning to slip out of the creature's grip, yelped in pain as she was yanked against its spikes which punctured her back and backside. The Red Queen began to scream.

'No, no, not my Colin! We had a deal, I did what you wanted. Give me back my Colin you son of a bitch!'

Jane sensed something fly past her and looked away from the now mouldy, but still wriggling and screeching, remains on the bed to see Clarissa fly into the wall. The sound of cracking bones brought her gaze back to the bed where she watched in fascination as yellow white bone tore and poked through the black suffocating mould his flesh had become and contracted limbs began to twist and snap like tree branches. Jane heard the glass window shatter, felt the cold wind sooth her aching joints and bleeding flesh, as one of the fiends from the garden roared as it leapt into the room. The room shook under their weight as Jane caught glimpses of at least four of the twisted fiends, one was the hell hound, another had an almost human face. Jane was momentarily terrified that she would be dropped onto Mr Smithson's mulch. But what had been the six clocks held her firmly as the room erupted in screams of terror and pain and blood splattered her and the wooden beast along with Mr Smithson in the bed. He no longer had a bottom jaw, his grey tongue lopped out and licked at the blood on his face, and for the first time, as his joints broke and twisted so that he was now a four legged beast, she saw Erazmus Nark, pulsing in the wreck. Suddenly she was no longer in the wooden embrace but passed onto something so cold that her teeth began to chatter. Suddenly she was stood in a puddle of wet robes before Richard who looked far more blood spattered than she felt. Still beside him, unharmed and unsoiled, was Dolly whom, without changing her facial expression, dropped to one knee with a series of clicks as if she too was clock work. Silently she stood before Richard and waited for him to say something. He always had something to say, he could charm himself out of anything. Instead of speaking, his mouth opened and closed, his bulging eyes staring wildly at the carnage around them. A loud scream, along with a lot of wet slurping noises, tore from the bed behind them.

Sounds like Woody is sucking Erazmus Nark up through a straw, thought Jane as a cold hand took her shoulder.

Looking around she saw Dolly, who now stood hand clamped on her shoulder, and the hell hound, grey and semi-transparent. Jane could see right through whatever accounted for his flesh at the workings within. This animal appeared far less Lovecraftian and much more anchored in the real world. It appeared to have fur, its head was long with snapping jaws and gave Jane the impression of a wolf, as did the rest of it, even if its size resembled more of a grizzly bear. The low growl that escaped its salivating jaws also anchored it firmly alongside Jane and the surviving cult that ran or crawled away from what they had assisted into the world. The fiend who Jane was now certain was responsible for pooing in Molly's boot, lowered its head so she could look directly into its red eyes and see the swirling depths within. Seeing the beast it had been before it was corrupted, Jane understood that it was a child of the land, seduced and twisted by it rather than absorbed into it, and that she was a child of the land also. The animal nuzzled its ice-like snout against her own nose and Jane noticed for the first time what the animal held in its jaws.

Silently she reached up and the beast allowed her to take it from its mouth. The slurping at the bed stopped and Jane looked around suspiciously. The large wooden creation was stood on the bed, a malevolent air about it, and Jane knew it watched her. Beside where the Red Queen had fallen stood a pale figure.

'Guess you kept your promise after all, didn't you?' Jane said to the malevolent figure that cracked its wooden joints and looked back at her.

Unwillingly she turned her back on it and faced Richard. Thinking of Rowena, Jane brought the hammer, her hammer, up.

'Marn, please, I love you.'

'You should have loved her then.'

With that, Jane brought the hammer down point first into Richard's skull and everything, including herself, seemed to howl at once.

Chapter 24

Twelve months later

Jane stood in the garden of Hacket house and tended to the newly growing seeds she'd managed to plant. It was early in the morning, before Atticus got up and insisted on doing all the even vaguely heavy work. He hadn't been there for the massacre. Not being a member of the Church of Hacket House he'd spent the evening getting legless in the empty pub along with other villagers who did not belong to the church. The church had been almost totally wiped out, including both Mr Hubbs, Mr Jonas, Mr Owen, Caroline, Molly, and Dora. In the morning after the ceremony, she and Atticus had gathered up the body parts and buried them in the little graveyard. They'd burnt the nursing bed. Dolly Hacket still hung around of course, a malevolent presence staring into space. Since Jane had cracked Richard's skull open and buried him with Nark, the woman had rightly kept her distance. Jane had spent many hours with Nark's library and was itching to try some of the spells and rituals herself when the time was right.

But she was pregnant now, barely enough to show but all the same. Atticus thought caution was the best policy regarding physical work and supernatural practices. She didn't know what the father was of course, it didn't matter, what mattered was getting Rowena back again. Standing in the garden by Grey's cave, as the beast snored within, Jane looked up at Hacket House. The building was pretty much the same as it had been the day she arrived. But it felt a million times brighter without the blight of Erazmus Nark and Clarissa's grim determination to get Colin back whatever the cost. She missed Dora and Molly, who had set up that social media account that brought Richard back into her life. There was no longer a mothers' group; the mother of the blonde baby had left the village along with her child when her husband had begun to go insane. Back when the pets had first started to go missing. It was a pity, Jane would have liked to join now.

Most of the village was dead, and those who weren't either disappeared or scuttled around like beetles exposed to the sun for the first time. Jane guessed the land had got tired of being worshiped and prayed to and decided it was time for new blood. And new blood was coming, every month or so someone new moved into the village. Attracted by too good to be true property prices and Clarissa, the Red Queen's charm. Jane still shuddered at her willingness to believe Mr Smithson's so called 'dementia'. Sometimes, as she laid in bed at night, she wondered how many Mr Smithson's were out there, branded as ill whilst really something far worse imprisoned them. Jane smiled to herself as Colin's transparent form stood on the step beside Clarissa who had been gaining weight. Together they looked out at the red land and her garden. They made such a good couple in the world at the bottom of the rabbit hole. Jane turned away and headed back to the cottage, feeling the pulse of the land come up through her boots.

Made in the USA
Middletown, DE
06 November 2020